GEO'S FORTUNE

Published by
PEACHTREE PUBLISHING COMPANY INC.
1700 Chattahoochee Avenue
Atlanta, Georgia 30318-2112
PeachtreeBooks.com

Text © 2025 by Amy B. Mucha
Jacket illustration © 2025 by Kelley McMorris

All rights reserved. No part of this publication may be reproduced, stored in a retrieval system, or transmitted in any form or by any means—electronic, mechanical, photocopy, recording, or any other—except for brief quotations in printed reviews, without the prior permission of the publisher.

Edited by Catherine Frank
Design and composition by Lily Steele

Printed and bound in March 2025 at Sheridan, Chelsea, MI, USA
10 9 8 7 6 5 4 3 2 1
First Edition
ISBN: 978-1-68263-671-8

Cataloging-in-Publication Data is available from the Library of Congress.

EU Authorized Representative: HackettFlynn Ltd, 36 Cloch Choirneal, Balrothery, Co. Dublin, K32 C942, Ireland. EU@walkerpublishinggroup.com

GEO'S FORTUNE

AMY B. MUCHA

Ω
PEACHTREE
ATLANTA

To Susie Wilde
and Wilde Writers everywhere

and to Ellen Manning
and all her magnificent Meerkats

I never could have done this without you.

CHAPTER 1

Probably for most kids, seeing their mom cry is a normal thing, or at least a not-so-horrible thing. Normal moms probably cry all the time. I can picture them now in their yoga pants, sniffling at baby wipe commercials, boo-hooing when their computers break down, or sobbing when their kid brings home an F on their report card.

But my mom isn't a normal mom. My mom is blue hair, tattoos, ripped jeans, and pierced everything. My mom is martial-arts, goth-girl, punk-rock chaotic. She doesn't exactly go for sappy television. She likes straight-up murder, the gorier the better. And when her computer breaks down? She takes it apart with a screwdriver and puts it back together again with extra memory.

Seriously, she didn't even cry when my dad died. At least, not that I remember. It was a long time ago. The point is, my mother, Rae Lynn Leoni? Does. Not. Cry.

Except, apparently, when it's the first week of summer vacation and we're in the middle of a massive heat wave, we have no central air, the house is falling apart, and oh, by the way, she's completely out of money.

"Wait, what?" I asked, staring at her hard.

It was nearly bedtime when she pulled me into her office (aka the laundry room) and sat me down in one of the folding chairs in front of her desk (aka the card table). She'd been crying so hard her eye makeup had leaked down her face making her look like one of those scary mime dudes. She'd borrowed money last year, she said. We were in financial trouble, way bigger than usual. Things were going to have to change.

"Change? Like how?" I asked, my whole body going alert.

"Like no more organic food," she said.

I exhaled. Who cared about that?

"And hitting thrift shops when we need new clothes," she added.

I waved my hand like I was batting away a fly. "All my clothes are trash anyway. Wearing someone else's throwaways would be an upgrade."

"Also, no more Grrrls Dates."

That one hit harder. Yes, calling them Grrrls Dates is completely embarrassing, but they'd been our monthly tradition since, well, forever. "No more pizza? No more movies and popcorn?"

"Not unless you believe in miracles," she said. "There's something else, too . . ." She looked like she was holding her breath a little bit. "It's my job. As in, I need to get one. A real one, not just contracting. A nine-to-five."

I blinked at her. "Like, in an office somewhere?"

She nodded, swallowing.

"But, Mom, I'm sure you'll get more contracts. You've always had plenty before."

"Yeah, before. When the economy tanked"—she looked away—"the gig market collapsed. If we're going to make it, I need something solid. With benefits. If I get an offer like that, I'm taking it."

My heart squeezed as I thought of how empty the house would feel with her gone every day. Then I noticed her face again. My mom wouldn't be crying just because of a stupid job. She was way tougher than that. "There's more, isn't there?" I asked, my stomach pooling with dread.

She swiped her eyes with her sleeve and sniffed. "The thing is there aren't a ton of jobs in this town. Not in my field—"

"Wait," I said, holding up my hands like I could keep her from saying it.

"I'm applying across the country," she finished.

You know how sometimes when scuba divers come to the surface too quick, something happens to the oxygen in their blood, and it makes their field of vision narrow to a pinprick? That's what happened to me, except it wasn't my vision. It was my everything. My whole world reduced to one tiny circle, and in the center of that circle was my mother, telling me she might take my entire life away.

"No," I said, swallowing my panic. "Absolutely not."

Her eyes filled up again.

Looking back, I should have known things were even worse than she was letting on. After all, we were living in the house my dad left us when he died, back when I was a toddler. Sure, it might be pretty run-down, but so what? It was the house he grew up in, and now it was ours. She wouldn't make us leave unless she had to. But I was in such a panic, all I could think is that I had to stop this from happening. No way was I leaving this house, this town, Alan, and most of all, Lana.

"Don't do it yet," I said, standing up so fast I bumped the table. "Just . . . hold on a minute. Stay right there. Don't move." I pounded across the chipped linoleum, slid around to the staircase, and flew up three creaky flights, careful to avoid the broken banister, because even when I am panicked, I am smart.

I ran into my room and threw open my closet door. Third shelf up, blue cash box. I quickly turned the code—13, 3, 31—and grabbed a thick, solid wad of perfectly rolled green. Twenties on the outside, then tens, then fives, ones in the middle. I didn't need to count it. I always knew exactly how much money I had.

I flew back downstairs and into the laundry room and tossed it to her. "Here. Take it."

The money bounced off the pixie tattoo on her arm and skidded across the card table, landing neatly against her computer keyboard. She stared at it.

"There's over three hundred dollars there," I said. "Three hundred and thirty-seven to be exact."

She kept staring, like it was a snake that could bite her. "Geo, I am not taking your money."

"Oh yes you are," I said. "It's my money. That means I spend it how I want. And I want to spend it on this."

She squeezed her eyes shut, then nodded. "It's a lot, but it's not enough to—"

"Duh!" I snorted, cutting her off. "I'm not five years old. I know that's not nearly enough to make a difference. My point is, I can make more. You know me, Mom. Making money is my thing. It's what I'm good at. And I have the whole summer ahead of me."

She opened her eyes. Her face was blotchy and soft. "You're only thirteen—"

I cut her off again, this time with a slap to the table. "Don't underestimate me. After all," I added, forcing a smile, "I'm your kid, right?"

She looked at me with an expression that was halfway between proud and heartbroken. "You're amazing, Georgia May Leoni. You know that?"

"Of course I do," I said, standing up to my full height of five foot nothing. "Just give me a few weeks. I'm going to bring in enough to keep us here."

She bit her lip. Then she reached out and took my hands in hers. "I'm not making any promises, but thank you."

I paused for a few moments while she gazed at me all gooey. Then I smiled sweetly, blinking. "By the way, Mom?"

"Yes?"

"Call me Butt Brain or Stink Bot or Fug Face. If you absolutely must, call me Geo. But do not *ever* call me Georgia May." I ended with a glare to show her I meant it.

She brushed some more tears away, but then she laughed. Her shoulders seemed to relax a tiny bit as she took my money, unrolled it, and smacked me with it softly on the side of my head. "All right, Stink Bot." She jammed it into a pocket of her cargo shorts and gave the lump a pat. "Every bit helps, so thank you."

I leaned in for a quick, fierce hug, then headed upstairs. My heart was pounding again as I climbed the three flights to my room, but this time it wasn't just from the exercise. We needed money, and I needed a plan.

I took out my phone and texted Lana. I put a 911, then wrote, "**playground tomorrow, 8am, bring breakfast.**"

CHAPTER 2

I popped awake the next morning, pumped for problem-solving. Lana and I had made tons of money in past summers, enough for me to buy my own phone and Fridgie, my air conditioner, and for her to buy an entire roomful of rocks. I was sure we could make enough so I wouldn't have to move. I yanked on yesterday's shorts and T-shirt, and pulled my hair back into a quick ponytail, or attempted to. My giant blond frizz-curls weren't quite long enough, and besides, they hated being tamed.

The old steps moaned as I flew down them in my flip-flops. "Playground!" I shouted toward the laundry room, before slamming through the screen door and pounding across the wood porch, hoping as always that today wasn't the day it decided to collapse underneath me. Taking the usual route past two-hundred-year-old oak trees and big fancy homes, I finally arrived, sweaty and panting, to the park where Lana and I spent most of our time.

It was eight a.m. on the dot but she was already there, spinning slowly on her favorite swing, the one closest to the enormous bright-yellow fiberglass stegosaurus we'd named Steggy. Yes, Steggy the Stegosaurus. It was a long time ago. We were five.

I stumbled toward her, wheezing dramatically as my stomach rumbled. "Made it. Breakfast?"

"Of course," she said, clutching her chest like I'd insulted her. She unzipped her overstuffed gray backpack and piled up a dozen mini cereal boxes on the bench next to the swing set. The sugary kind, of course. That's why Lana brings the food: Breakfast at my house meant kale smoothies or a box of gluten-free sugar-free vegan cardboard kibbles, whereas Lana's dad always bought us all the little boxes of sugar bombs we could want. It's not like a diet of junk food had done Lana any harm. She was close to six feet tall, solid and strong, with long dark hair as thick as a rope.

"So what's going on?" she asked, tearing open the first box.

"It's not good," I said, wiping sugar dust off my cheek. As I explained the situation, she stopped chewing and slowly put down her box.

"You can't move," she said when I finished. "You *can't*."

"I know!" I said. "That's why we need to figure out a way to make money. Big money."

She nodded vigorously. "We can sell rocks." This was not exactly a shocking suggestion. Lana was capital O obsessed with rocks and would like nothing more than to work them into our summer somehow. But my priority was money, not rocks. "That was fine when we were eight. But we need real money now, not little-kid money."

"I didn't mean selling pieces of gravel," she said, shaking her head. "I meant selling MY rocks. My entire collection. It's worth a lot."

"Oh, Lana," I said, my heart melting. She had been building up that collection forever. "Never in a million years would I let you sell your rock collection."

"I would sell it in a second if it meant you could stay."

My heart melted even more, but I shook my head firmly. "No."

She bit her lip and went back to thinking. "Giant garage sale?"

"Your dad would never let us, and we've got nothing worth selling anyway," I said. "But even if we did, a garage sale is a one-shot deal. What we need is income. Regular, reliable pay."

"Too bad for child labor laws."

"You're telling me," I said, disgusted. Like I couldn't serve coffee or sell French fries. "If we could fake being sixteen, we could at least pull in minimum wage."

"Sadly, you look like you're nine."

I play-smacked her. "Yeah, well, if you put makeup on, you'd look twenty-three. If we averaged our looks, we'd be sixteen."

"And if you averaged our intelligence..."

I smacked her again before she could finish and laughed for the first time that day. It was rare for Lana to snark me twice in a row. I was proud of her. But the feeling fizzled fast, my laugh ending in a sigh. "It doesn't matter anyway. Those jobs would only get us what, like ten dollars an hour? I need way more than that."

"How much?" she asked.

"10K?" I answered.

Her eyes went big. "Ten thousand dollars?" she asked.

"I know it's way more than we've ever made before, but come on, it's us. We can do this."

She pressed her lips together for a moment, then got practical. "Okay, there are ten and a half weeks left of summer. Let's call it seventy days. Even if we take no days off, like, *at all*, we'd still need to make over a hundred and forty dollars a day."

"A hundred and forty a day? That's totally doable!"

"Sure," she said, rolling her eyes. "Easy." She did some more math in her head. "We might come close if we did the babysitting club again, but we'd need three times as many sitters."

I made a face. "No way." We'd made decent money watching kids the summer before, but it had ended badly. I strongly suspected none of the overprotective parents would trust me with their kid again after the whole kitchen mixer cookie dough incident. I still say if an eight-year-old kid is too dumb to know he's not supposed to stick his hand into a moving machine part, he gets what's coming to him.

We went over all the other stuff we'd done before that: the tie-dye business, candy reselling, the online merch store. All had made decent money, but we needed to do better than decent.

"Maybe something with social media?" Lana ventured, chewing the side of her nail.

"No," I said firmly. I didn't do social media, and that was that. "I wish we could do that homework scam plan I came up with last fall. Alas, it's summer."

"And also," said Lana, glaring, "it's cheating."

"Cheating schmeating," I said, waving her away. Lana was always trying to make me a better person, but at times like this, money was more important than morals. "Anyway, these are old ideas. We need new ones. Bigger ones. Not pebble-sized ideas. We need boulders."

Lana brightened like she always did when I used rock metaphors. "These ideas are lightweight, like pumice," she said, making her voice sound like an ancient wise man. "We need heavy, like granite."

"They are soft like . . ."

"Talc," she finished.

"We need tough like . . ."

"Rubies!"

"These are cheap like . . ."

"Sandstone."

"We need rich like . . ."

"Gold!" Lana jumped up, pumping her fist in the air.

"Rubies and gold!" we cheered. But after that burst of geeked-out excitement, we rock-slid straight into silence. No ideas came, not then, and not the whole rest of the day either. Finally, we collapsed back where we'd started, on the bench next to Steggy, feeling low and heavy, like clay.

"What is going on with me?" Usually ideas came as easy as sparks popping off a wood fire. I wiped my forehead on my T-shirt sleeve. "It's this stinking heat."

"We just need to sleep on it," Lana said, then glanced at her phone. "I should be getting home."

"Yeah," I said. "I'll walk you."

Lana lived three blocks from the playground too, but in the opposite direction from me, and even though we're close our neighborhoods were completely different. I lived in the old, posh part of town, where the only shabby house was mine. Lana lived across the four-lane road on the other side of the park. Picture row upon row of exactly the same house, over and over again, with no trees at all. It didn't have a ton of charm, but the houses were decently big and they all had central air-conditioning. Huge bonus if you ask me.

Not that it helped Lana much. Her house wasn't old and hot and falling apart like mine, but it hardly mattered because every square inch of it was bursting with trash. Her dad's a super nice guy with a steady job, but he's also a bona fide hoarder. Lana doesn't even let me inside anymore, which is why I only walk her as far as the busy street.

"We'll come up with something tomorrow," she said, waiting for the light to change. "I'm sure of it."

"Eight a.m.?"

"Eight a.m.," she said as the pedestrian sign turned white. I watched as she dashed across the road, her long brown hair flopping on her sturdy back, then I gave her a quick thumbs-up before she disappeared into the rows of homes.

CHAPTER 3

I got back to my stifling house and quickly yanked the screen door shut behind me, hoping no mosquitoes followed me inside.

"Hey, Stink Face," called my mom from the laundry room. "Is that you? Dinner's on the counter. Want to grab it and binge a miniseries with me?"

"No thanks," I called back. Watching a show with both of us crowded around her tiny laptop didn't sound too enticing. After I finished eating the lentil salad she'd left me, I headed upstairs to think. Roughly four thousand hours later, I punched my fist into my mattress. My whole room felt hot with failure. Usually when I decided to make money, ideas came fast. Why, when I needed it most, was my mind a blank?

I got up to check my air conditioner for the sixteenth time. I patted his smooth, metallic side. "Come on, Fridgie.

Don't give up on me now." One week into summer vacation, and our relationship was getting fraught. He was my first big purchase, bought when I was ten, and since then we'd spent many deliciously cool nights together. But that night my room was heating up despite his best efforts, and instead of his usual chilled air, Fridgie was choking out a grinding noise. He seemed, like me, ready to give up.

I pressed my forehead into his moaning self and sighed.

"Think, think, think," I said, gently banging my head against his metallic side.

It was no use. I sank down against the wall until I landed on the old, brown carpet. I sat for a few long minutes, and then did something I'd never done before in my entire life.

I prayed.

Me. Born to a skeptic, raised by a skeptic, scorner of all unscientific, unproven beliefs. Praying.

At least, I think it was praying. Is it still called that if you're talking to your dead dad instead of a god? Because that's what I did.

"Dad," I said, speaking out into the nothingness of my mind. "I know praying is dumb and if you still had eyes you'd be rolling them at me. But I don't care. Mom and I need you. We need money. Real money. So, please, help me figure out how to make it."

I paused, not sure how to end it. I knew most people ended prayers with *Amen*, but that felt weird. Mom had always said that my dad scoffed at faith. That what he prized above anything was a nice tall glass of logic. So after a minute, I added, "And yes, it's completely embarrassing asking a dead guy for help, but you have to admit that it never hurts to hedge your bets. I promise I'm still smart and skeptical. I'm just desperate is all. Love, Geo."

I took a deep breath and let it out. And I had to admit, I felt weirdly better. Lighter and less worried. Maybe this was why people prayed. Because it felt good.

I stood up, stretched and yawned, and noticed something. Fridgie had stopped moaning. He was whirring like a well-oiled machine half his age. I put my hand up to his vent and felt a stream of cold air. I nearly collapsed in gratitude. I fell back onto my bed, and this time I'm pretty sure I was asleep before my head hit the pillow.

CHAPTER 4

I woke the next morning to the sound of a car door slamming in the driveway and a low beam of sunlight slanting through my room like a giant orange glow stick. When I felt the rumble of the garage door opening, I grabbed my phone off my nightstand and groaned. It was way-too-early o'clock. Who on earth was here?

I was lying in bed trying to decide if my curiosity or my tiredness was going to win, when I heard soft footsteps coming up the stairs to my room. A moment later, there was an even softer knock at my door.

"Yes?" I asked, squinting as I picked my head up off the pillow.

"It's me," whispered my mom. "Can I come in?" One of the great things about my mom is that she is big into Respecting My Space. That means she hardly ever comes up to my room and would never in a million years open the door without permission. But that meant when she did come up, it was usually important.

"Of course," I said, sitting up. "What's going on?"

She had a funny, lopsided grin and if I didn't know better, I might even say her eyes were shining with tears. "Sorry, I couldn't wait . . . Alan just dropped by. He found something and wanted to show me in person." Alan had been my dad's best friend in college, then after my dad died, Alan became best friends with my mom. He also became the closest thing I've ever had to a dad.

"What is it?" I asked, rubbing my eyes.

She lifted her phone in the air. "It's a video of your dad. A new one!"

"Dad?" Whoa. My head got so light I felt dizzy. I'd memorized every video I had of my dad word for word a long time ago; it never occurred to me that we'd find a new one. And definitely not the very next morning after I'd asked him for help.

My mom's grin got even more crooked as she held the screen out to me. "Look!"

Sure enough, there was my dad, standing on a stage in front of a giant banner that read SKEPTICS SOCIETY CONVENTION.

"Wait till you see Alan," my mom continued, sitting next to me. "He's on it too. He looks like a baby!" She pressed a spot on the screen and the video started to play, showing my dad clapping and smiling as a nerdy teenaged Alan walked nervously toward the podium. When Alan stuck out his hand for a proper handshake, my dad pulled him in for a bear hug instead, then left his arm draped around Alan's neck, making everyone laugh.

Even though they were best friends, I'd never seen them in a video together before. All at once, it hit me: Here was my dad, the guy who should've raised me, but couldn't, together with the guy who didn't need to raise me, but did. My chest squeezed so hard it took my breath away.

My throat was so tight I had to clear it. "Do you mind if I watch it alone?" I asked, hoping I wasn't hurting her feelings. "It's just . . . it's a lot."

"Of course," she said, giving me a long, squeezy side hug. "I'll text you the link." She tapped on her phone, then stood to leave, pausing at the door. She wasn't shedding any tears, but her voice was as rough as mine as she said, "I wish you could have known him. Oh, Geo, he had such confidence and charisma. You remind me more and more of him all the time."

The moment she shut the door I clicked the link. Whoever recorded the video had started it right in the middle of the speech my dad was giving. "As a species," he was saying, "humans are easy to manipulate, willing to adopt the most ridiculous beliefs as long as those beliefs provide them with the illusion of order and control . . ."

My mom was right. My dad was a natural performer, full of confidence and not the least bit nervous onstage. He even put on different funny voices, and at one point said "oh my gourd" instead of "oh my god," cracking the whole place up. Hearing that gave me a jolt—saying "oh my gourd" and "gourd bless you" had always been my and Alan's thing. Hearing my dad say it made me realize that it had been his thing first, and if he hadn't died, it would have been *our* thing. I'm not embarrassed to admit that the thought made my eyes sting with tears.

He continued, going on about how gullible people are and how they'll buy anything if you sell it to them right. Then, right at the 33:33 mark, he paused dramatically, gripped the podium, and stared straight into the camera like he knew I was there. "Know what I'd do if I needed money fast? I'd become a psychic." He paused while the audience twittered. "You laugh. But psychic scammers make fast, easy money; at least, the good ones do. People will believe anything if you assert it with confidence." He leaned back, smiling. "That's why they call it a 'con.' It's a confidence game. I'm telling you: I could start a fortune-telling business tomorrow and be living large by the end of summer."

My heart thumped in my chest. I dropped the phone like it was hot and sat stock-still until I realized I wasn't breathing and had to gasp for air.

Once the world stopped spinning, I picked the phone up and texted two words to Lana with shaking fingers.

"Park. Now."

CHAPTER 5

Lana pulled her long braid in front of her and twirled it in her fingers like she always did when she got nervous. "You think we're going to make ten thousand dollars . . . fortune-telling?"

"I don't think it," I said, tossing a handful of Cap'n Crunch into my mouth. "I'm sure of it."

"Okaaaay," she said, her brow creasing in the early-morning light. "You do realize that fortune-telling generally involves . . . telling fortunes?"

I waved my hand. "Fortune tellers are nothing more than con artists. And I"—I thumped my chest—"am a natural scammer."

"My confidence is not increasing," she said.

"Think about it. You said we have seventy days until school starts, right?"

"More or less."

"Let's say we charge ten dollars per client. We'd only need fourteen clients per day. That's nothing!"

"Fourteen is not nothing," she said, frowning. "If anything, it's a lot."

"You're forgetting to count repeat customers."

"You think people are going to pay you to scam them twice?"

"More than twice. People are gullible, Lana. We'll have regulars in no time!"

Lana poured some Froot Loops into her mouth and chewed. "Okay, but, like, how? Where?"

I felt my brain light up with tingles. Now that I knew the what, the how came quickly. "Right here," I said. "We're here all the time anyway, and there're plenty of kids. Rich ones. It's perfect!"

"Here?" she asked, looking dubiously at the bench. "How will we get them to come?"

"Do you still have that card table and folding chairs? The ones we used for a lemonade stand?"

"Of course." She wrinkled her nose. "Assuming I can dig them out."

"So we'll set them up right here, in the shade by Steggy. We'll drape silky scarves all over it and burn incense and stuff. We can even dress up! Big hoop earrings, long beaded necklaces, tons of eyeliner. Or—ooh! Maybe a turban!"

"Definitely not a turban," said Lana, giving me a sharp look. "That's offensive to actual turban-wearing people."

"You're right," I said quickly. "No turban." This is exactly why Lana is so good for me: She stops me from offending people at least once a week. "But we should get a prop to do the readings with. Like those tarot card thingies, or a crystal ball."

"Who's going to pay for all this stuff?"

My face fell as I remembered giving all my money to my mom.

"I have thirty-five dollars," said Lana quickly. "We can get a few things with that."

I squeezed her arm. "Thanks, Lana. And don't worry, I'll get that money back to you fast, with interest."

"No way," she said. "You keep it. It's for you and your mom."

I waved as I slid off the bench, filled with sugar and certainty. "We're going to make so much it's not going to matter. Come on!"

She tossed her braid behind her and jumped up, ready for action. "Where are we going?"

I pointed over her shoulder. "To the Sucker Store!"

CHAPTER 6

Lana knew exactly what I was talking about, and no, it's not a store that sells suckers. They sell *to* suckers. Its windows were filled with candles, crystal skulls, and books with titles like *Channeling Your Inner Goddess* and *Meeting Your Angel Guide in Ten Easy Steps*. I'd been making fun of that New Age nitwit store from the moment it opened. It was guaranteed to have exactly the kind of ridiculous nonsense that would make us seem legit.

But instead of getting excited with me, Lana plopped back down on the bench. "I don't think so."

"Oh, come on. It's perfect!"

"You go ahead. I'll get the card table."

"Lana, you can't carry that by yourself. Besides, you don't want to miss this." I put my finger next to my temple and spun it in circles. "That place is going to be hilarious. It'll be fun!"

But Lana just sat there, looking nervous and stubborn at once.

I stared at her. "What's going on? You're not actually spooked by that store, are you? You're smarter than that. Now come on." I tugged her arm until she finally stood up and let me drag her across the busy road and past the gas station, the mini-mart, and several blocks of red-bricked buildings, until we reached the center of town.

"Closed," said Lana, trying to hide her relief.

I squinted at the sign. "Incense and Sensibility. It's the place for incense, all right. I'm not sure about the sensible part, though."

"Actually, sensibility doesn't mean being sensible; it's about feelings." She looked at me pointedly. "It's about being *sensitive*."

"Oh," I said. "So it's the opposite of sensible, then."

Lana rolled her eyes, but smiled a little, too. Then she turned back toward the park. "Okay, it's closed. Let's go."

"Seriously, what is up with you?" I cupped my hands around my eyes and peered inside. I couldn't see much, just a bookshelf and a table covered in about a million different crystals. "Lana, check out all these rocks! Hey, someone's in there." I waved. "They're coming!"

Lana looked like she was about to bolt, so I grabbed her arm and held it as the door to the store opened. There was a tinkling of a bell and a girl our age poked her head out.

Nearly as tiny as me but with wispy hair and giant anime eyes, she was wearing a long flowy skirt, chunky sandals, a tank top, and a beaded necklace. In other words, your basic New Age hippie poster child. But more than anything else, here's what I saw: This girl was way pretty but didn't know it. She had no confidence at all. I could tell by her shoulders. It's amazing the things you can learn, just by looking at shoulders.

"Um, hi!" she said. "My aunt's in the shower but you can come in." She spoke in a rushed way, blushing pink as though she'd said something embarrassing. "Let me turn the lights on." She disappeared into the back of the store, leaving the door ajar.

I followed, dragging Lana behind me, then immediately coughed. What was that smell?

"Sorry!" called the girl as the lights popped on. "Aunt Liv just smudged. It's still a bit strong."

"Aha," I said. "That's exactly what we need. Smudge!"

"Oh, okay . . . um, do you mean sage?" asked the girl as she came back into the room.

"Yeah, that's what I said. Sage."

"It's over here. My aunt grows it herself, so don't worry, it's ethically sourced. And actually, I'm not supposed to call it smudging anymore, so forget I said that. We say 'space clearing' now." She reached into a cardboard box filled with small bundles of dried plants tied with a thin red string and pulled one out eagerly. "Um, do you need to clear some negative energy?"

I deserved an Academy Award for keeping my face straight through all of that. "Definitely," I said, pointing over my shoulder. "It's my friend here. She's got, like, *tons* of negative energy."

The girl glanced at Lana with a wrinkled forehead, trying to figure out if I was joking or not. Lana's nostrils flared. "So," I continued, "what's your name?"

"Feather," she said, taking the herb bundle over to the glass counter.

This time I clamped my mouth shut so hard my teeth ached. Did she say Feather? FEATHER? If my business instincts weren't so strong, I'd have been rolling on their patchouli-scented rug laughing. But I behaved: After all, this girl wasn't just a potential client. She might be my first, my best, and my single most valuable client. Who was better positioned than her to spread the word to other gullible dunkheads? Heck, I could probably even talk her into hanging a flyer in the shop for free!

I stuck out my hand. "I'm Geo Leoni. It's nice to meet you." I'm a fan of a good handshake. Adults love it and kids get thrown by it; either way it works to my advantage. Feather blinked at it for a second, then shook. As expected, her hand was soft and limp. I gave it a few solid pumps. "We're setting up a fortune-telling stand."

"A . . . um, fortune-telling?"

"That's right. You heard me. I can see the future."

"Oh! Sorry, it's just I've only ever heard people call it that as a joke. You mean you're a psychic, right?"

"You got it in one," I said, flying past my mistake without missing a beat. "In fact, I'm in the market for a new crystal ball."

Feather paused again. Then she laughed. "You *are* being funny. For a second I thought you were serious. As if real psychics use crystal balls and wear scarves and hoop earrings and stuff." She rolled her eyes, and I made a mental note to skip the crystal ball, scarves, and earrings. Then she leaned forward and asked, "So, what's your clair?"

Uh-oh. I kept the smile plastered on my face. "My . . . what?"

"You know, clair. Clairvoyance, clairaudience, clairsentience, claircognizance. I'm clairsentient, myself. Not that I'm all that good at it, or anything," she added with yet another blush. "I don't practice enough."

"Oh, that," I said with a wave of my hand. "I'm all of them."

Her eyes widened. "All of them? For real?"

"Yeah." I shrugged. "I don't mean to brag, but I'm, like, *super* gifted."

Lana's lips had set into a thin line but thankfully Feather was too busy gushing to notice. "That's so cool!" Wistfully, she added, "I haven't met anyone else our age who cares about stuff like this."

A sudden knowledge flooded into me. There was a reason I had never seen this strange girl before. There was a reason she was new in town, suddenly here in this shop with her aunt. I took my hunch and ran with it, leaning in close. "That's why you're here," I whispered.

"You can see that?" she whispered back.

"Easily," I said, ignoring the daggers Lana was shooting me. "You came here to find more people like you. To feel like you belong." Easy as that, I had her. She was practically panting to hear more. My dad was right. This scamming stuff was easy! "Come by our stand tomorrow for a full reading. It's only ten bucks."

Feather squeezed her hands together. "I'd love that!"

We heard some noises in the back room. Lana tugged at my T-shirt. "Let's go!" she hissed.

"I'm not done," I hissed right back. "Never mind her," I said to Feather. "She'll be better after the . . ." Shoot. What was it again? "Smoodging."

"Space clearing," she corrected shyly.

"Right," I said, trying to keep my expression straight. "The space clearing." Lana jabbed me hard enough to hurt. If I didn't leave soon, she was going to bruise my ribs. "We'll just look a little more . . . Ow! Okay, fine! I mean, we'd better get going. We'll be in the park four blocks from here. Be there tomorrow, okay?"

Feather's eyes were shining. "I will," she promised. As we turned to go, I heard another noise in the back room. "Wait!" said Feather, as Lana grabbed my arm and pulled. "You almost forgot the sage!"

I yanked myself out of Lana's grasp and turned back. Coming down the hall behind Feather was a woman who was dressed just like her, from the tank top down to the hippie skirt and sandals. But this woman had freckles sprinkled across her cheeks, bright green eyes, and caramel-colored waves bouncing around her face.

And her shoulders? They weren't insecure at all.

She swept into the room and focused her sparkling eyes first on me, then above me. Her smile grew big and warm. "Lana!" she said. "I've been telling Feather all about you."

CHAPTER 7

For several seconds, no one moved.

The lady with the freckles was still smiling at Lana, but as the silence grew, her smile turned into more of a question. Finally, Lana spoke, her voice sounding high and forced. "Uh, Liv, this is my friend Geo. Geo, this is Liv. She, um, owns the store."

My entire mind was a question mark, which was bad, because this lady seemed sharp. She turned her bright, piercing eyes on me. They seemed to take in all of me, every last bit. If she saw through me, my business was kaput.

"Nice to meet you," I said, sticking out my hand. "Great store."

Liv's handshake was nothing like Feather's. Her grip was firm but gentle, and totally encompassing. Warmth seemed to shine out through every part of her, even her hands.

"Any friend of Lana's is a friend of mine," she said. "And I'm so glad you both met Feather! She flew in yesterday. In fact, I was hoping you could show her around town?"

Behind me, Lana made a small choking noise. Liv's eyes shifted off mine and grew concerned. "Lana? Are you okay?"

She was right to ask. Lana was looking downright green. "She had too much sugar for breakfast," I said quickly, then, glad for the excuse to get the heck out of there, added, "I'd better take her home."

"Let me get my keys. I'll give you a ride," said Liv, looking at Lana hard.

"No, we're fine! It's not far at all, and trust me, you don't want her upchucking in your car." I hauled Lana toward the door, not giving Liv any chance to argue. "Come by the park tomorrow, Feather," I called as we bumped out the door. "You can't miss us; just look for the yellow dinosaur."

"I will!" she shouted as the door clanged shut behind us.

I kept my game face on all the way to the gas station. Then I stopped and spun toward Lana. "What the junk? What. The. JUNK?" My business self had clamped down on my feelings while we were in the shop. Now they were exploding and I felt hot as a fireball. "You made me look like an idiot back there!"

Lana opened and closed her mouth like a guilty fish.

I started walking again, fast. She followed silently, like a guilt balloon on a string. "No wonder you didn't want to go there. You weren't scared, you just didn't want me figuring out that you and the owner are the new peanut butter and jelly, apparently. You've obviously spent plenty of time in that shop." I stopped and put my hands on my hips. "Tell me the truth, Lana: Are you into all that stupid New Age hippie garbage?"

And right there, in full view of the cars at the gas pumps, into the gnarled roots of a stubby sidewalk tree, Lana leaned over and barfed.

I'd seen her do it before. Like the time we tried to clean her kitchen as a surprise for her dad. He's usually a super nice guy, but that day, he flipped out on us. "Never touch my stuff, ever again," he screamed. That time, she ran outside and threw up in the bushes at the side of her house. Another time she threw a rock for fun and accidentally hit a boy in the head. She was puking before she had a chance to see that he was okay.

But she'd never thrown up because of me. As her Technicolor breakfast poured out of her, all my anger poured out with it. I vowed right then and there that Lana would never barf because of me, ever again.

When she was done, I reached out and gave her a couple of stiff pats on her back. "Are you okay?"

She wiped her mouth with her sleeve. Her eyes were streaming with tears. "Only if you don't hate me," she said after a few jagged breaths.

I would have hugged her, except who wants to hug someone who just threw up? So I gave her a couple more pats instead. "Of course I don't hate you. I was royally freaked out is all. I mean, you lied to me, Lana."

"I'm sorry," she said, slumping. "I . . . I've been going there for rocks." I closed my eyes, remembering the shelves full of crystals. Of course it was the rocks. How could I be so dumb? Duh! "I saw them in the window one day," she continued, "right after they opened. Liv knows more about rocks than anyone I've ever met." Lana dragged her toe in the dirt. "She's actually really smart."

I snorted. "*That* lady? Smart?" Then I thought back to her eyes, and the way they had looked right through me. Even though it didn't make any sense at all, I had to admit Liv had the eyes of a smart person.

"She has a degree in geophysics," said Lana.

Now it was my turn to open my mouth like a fish. "Geophysics? That's what you always say you want to study!"

"Exactly," said Lana. "And she's nice, too."

We didn't say anything else till we'd reached our bench. I was glad to see some color had returned to her cheeks. When we sat down, she groaned, leaning her head down into my shoulder. "I can't believe I vomited in front of the gas station with a million cars driving by." She shuddered, then looked up, her face twisted into a question mark. "We walked away and left it there. Is that okay?"

"Of course," I said decisively. "There are only two options when it comes to throw-up. You clean it up, or you walk away.

When it comes to neon rainbow gas station sidewalk barf? You definitely walk away."

She laughed, then put her hand on her stomach. "Is it weird that I'm hungry?"

"Nah. But maybe let's eat something healthy this time. Come on." I stood up and offered her my hand. "Let's go to my house."

As we walked through the park, one last question still nagged at me. "Why didn't you tell me you were going to that store?"

She pressed her lips together and said nothing.

"You knew I'd make fun of you," I said, my heart sinking. She didn't say yes, and she didn't say no. She didn't need to. I stopped walking. "It's occurring to me that I might be kind of a jerk sometimes."

"Yeah, but not to me, usually," she said in a small voice.

My heart sank. "I'm really, really sorry."

"That's okay," she said. But as we started walking again, guilt gnawed at my insides.

"I won't make fun of that store anymore. And I won't make fun of . . . What's the owner's name? Lib? Love?"

"Liv."

"Right. Liv. Even if she does believe in magic, which makes no sense at all for someone who studied science. And I'll even try to not make fun of Feather. Though, seriously, that name?"

Lana tried to keep her face straight, but couldn't. "It's a pretty ridiculous name," she admitted, grinning. "But she did seem kind of nice."

I thought back to Feather. There were a lot of words I would have used to describe her. Naive. Gullible. Insecure. Shy. Scared. Probably vacant as a sinkhole. And yes, nice. "Agreed."

"So you'll be nice back to her?" Lana double-checked.

Heck, being nice to that girl made plain good business sense. I held my hand in a pledge. "Promise."

CHAPTER 8

Lana felt much better after eating a proper breakfast, so when we were done we walked to her house to gather the card table, chairs, and easel. She made me wait at the curb, as usual, while she dug everything out. She even grabbed a giant, colorful tapestry with gold and purple fringe. It had a few holes and stains on it and smelled like ear cheese, but it would look okay once it was draped over the table. And that homemade sage stuff would help cover the stink.

We hauled everything to the park in a red wagon and set it up to see how it looked. I stood back and frowned. The tapestry added a nice touch, but something was definitely missing. The easel was still blank, but it was more than that. "Too bad crystal balls are out of style," I said. "It would help if the table weren't so empty."

"We could have Feather bring us some tarot cards."

"No way. I have no idea how to use those things. She'd see through me in a second."

Lana dug into the pocket of her shorts and pulled out a small chunk of slightly sparkly dark gray rock. She placed it in the center of the table and grinned. "There, some magnetite. It's magnetic, so maybe it'll attract customers?"

"Perfect," I said, laughing. "That's exactly what it needed."

"There's more where that came from," she teased.

"Why not?" I joked back, spreading out my arms. "The more the better."

She pulled out another rock, placing it next to the magnetite with a flourish. "That's my piece of flint. Ta-da!" she announced. The flint was a pale, almost colorless gray with smooth, glassy surfaces. Something about it drew me in, until I found myself reaching out and grasping it. It felt cold and hard in my palm.

"Careful," cautioned Lana. "It's sharp. Flint is what they made weapons out of in prehistoric times. It's not surgically sharp like obsidian, but it can still cut like a knife."

Out of nowhere a small breeze kicked up, and, despite the heat of the day, a shiver worked its way up my spine. For some reason, a crystal-clear image of Jade Sinclair popped up, so sudden and startling I flinched. Why on earth had *she* come to mind? I barely knew her, at least not personally. She was a social media influencer wannabe, and Alan had been dating her mother the last few months. He'd tried to get us to hang out, but we had nothing in common and didn't even go to the same school. And yet there she was, her sharp face hovering in the air in front of me, looking as real and as hard as the rock in my hand.

"It's interesting besides that, too," Lana was saying, staring at the flint as I held it. "It sparks if you hit it against something hard. That's why they used it to start fires before matches were invented." She kept going, but I'd stopped listening because Jade's image was still in front of me, except now her honey-colored eyes were turning a sinister, glowing orange. They got brighter and more intense until they were sending out sparks, the kind that happen when a log falls into a fire. Soon showers of sparks were falling from her face and hair, until BOOM, it felt like my entire brain burst into flames.

I gasped, dropping the flint like it had burned me. "Are you okay?" asked Lana, peering from my hands to my face. "It didn't cut you, did it?"

"No . . ." I started, flushing with heat and embarrassment. Had spending five minutes in Liv's woo-woo shop turned me into some kind of weirdo who had visions? I shook my head. Absolutely not. Not now, not ever. So instead I laughed, trying to make it sound natural. "I was just having a weird daydream."

"About?"

"About all the money we're going to make, duh. It's going to be amazing."

"Hmm," she said. She took the flint back, frowned for a second, then brightened. "I'm going to bring my pegmatite instead. If anything would bring us money luck, it's that. It's pretty, too; my specimen even has garnets in it."

"Definitely bring it," I said, and not only because it would make her happy. We really could use something for the table, and I might be a skeptic, but that doesn't mean I'm above a good luck charm. I stood back, picturing a big, pretty rock sitting in the center of the table. Something about the image tugged at me like it was trying to get my attention. I turned it around in my head as it danced right at the edges of my thoughts, like a tease.

Then, all at once, I had it. The idea was so good it made prickles run all the way up to my scalp.

"Lana, don't just bring one rock, bring ALL your rocks! Anyone can fake being boring, ordinary psychics. We're going to be something different. Something new. Something way, way better." I spread my arms wide with a flourish.

"We're going to be Rock Readers."

CHAPTER 9

Some ideas are so good they move through your body like living things. And this was a live one, no question. Goose bumps were shivering from my head all the way down to my toes and back again. I didn't need to sell Lana on the idea, obviously; she lit up like a glow stick just hearing about it. We spent the rest of the day at my house planning everything out, and by dinner I was bursting with certainty. Somehow, I just knew this plan was going to work.

I practically bounced into the kitchen, where my mom was standing in front of the stove, stirring a big steaming pot.

"There you are!" she said. "Right on time." She forked a huge heap of pasta onto a plate, then slopped a big ladle of sauce all over it and handed it to me. "Good day?"

"Crazy," I gushed, sitting down and waving the steam off my plate. Then I got a whiff. It smelled different, somehow.

Not bad, but definitely not our usual. It hit me that my mom was probably trying out a cheaper brand of sauce to save money. "It smells amazing," I said. "Even better than before. So . . . how much paper do you have in your printer?"

She laughed. "Someone's a little hyper. What do you need paper for?"

"Lana and I are going to make flyers."

"Flyers? Old-school!"

"Exactly," I said. "No one ever gets paper mail. That's why it's going to work. We're going to hang them everywhere, and put one in the mailbox of every house in town." I unfolded a piece of paper from my back pocket and thrust it toward her. She took it and read aloud:

ASK THE ROCK READERS!
~~ THE ROCKS REVEAL ALL!! ~~
YOUR FUTURE!

MONEY!

FORTUNE!

LOVE!

ROMANCE!

GRADES!

SPORTS!

MAGIC!

LUCK!

AND MORE!

> . . . ONLY $10 PER READING!!
> ***MONEY-BACK GUARANTEE***
> "GEO CHANGED MY LIFE!"
> "ROCK READINGS ARE WORTH $100 AT LEAST!"
> "TRUST ME, YOU WON'T REGRET IT, GET A ROCK READING TODAY!"
> OPEN DAILY
> IN THE PARK NEXT TO THE DINOSAUR.

Mom's eyebrows shot up, making her row of silver eyebrow piercings stick out in funny directions. "Rock Reading?" Then she smothered a smile. "'Geo changed my life'?"

I swallowed some milk. "I change lives every day."

"'Worth a hundred dollars at least'?"

"More like a thousand," I said.

"Hmmm," she said. "You do understand that being a psychic is a real thing? Like, people do it professionally? And you"—she poked my arm—"don't know the first thing about it."

"Oh, come on," I said, rolling my eyes. "Psychics aren't real. They're either scammers or boneheads. Don't pretend like you don't agree."

"You sound exactly like . . ." A light seemed to turn on behind her eyes. "Ohhhhh . . . that's where this is coming from. Your father's video."

"I'm taking Dad's advice." I shrugged. "Because he's right."

"Is he, though?" she said, putting the paper down.

"About psychics being con artists? Of course he is." I sighed. "You don't truly believe in any of that hocus-pocus, do you?"

But she just tilted her head and said, "Maybe, maybe not?"

Ugh. Sometimes getting a solid answer out of my mother was like trying to put smoke in a box. "Did you used to drive Dad crazy, too?"

Her smile turned mischievous. "Maybe?"

"Well, anyway," I continued. "We're doing it, and we're going to make a bundle. You'll see."

"That's part of what worries me," she said. "The idea of you scamming people for money, it's—"

"Genius?"

"Not the word I was going for. Look. You know I'm not going to tell you what to do. But I will ask you to give it some thought."

"I don't see what the big deal is," I said. "If people are dumb enough to hand money to a fortune teller, that's their problem, not mine. It's not like I'm forcing them."

"Yes, but by pretending to be something you're not, you're lying to them. You're cheating them. You're also being extremely judgmental about other people's beliefs. Is that really the kind of person you want to be?"

The kitchen got quiet while I gave it some thought. I had to admit that it didn't sound too good when she spelled it out like that. For a few short moments, I wondered if we should go back to the drawing board. Honestly, I probably would have, if the idea had been mine. But it hadn't. "This idea was Dad's, and he can't be wrong."

My mom blinked, then rubbed her eyes. "Stink Face, your dad was young in that video, very young—"

"Young and smart, like me. Look, I hear you. I do. But loads of kids get, like, twenty-dollar allowances every single week. Ten dollars is chump change to them. And in return, we'll give them at least ten dollars of entertainment, probably more. Plus, we're offering a money-back guarantee! If they feel like we cheated them, we'll repay them every penny, and that's the truth."

Slowly, she nodded. "Okay, but do me a favor: Pay attention to how you're feeling when you're doing this. If it feels wrong, notice that. Don't dismiss it. Agreed?"

"Agreed," I said, squirming a bit in my chair. My mom might have a policy of not telling me what to do, but she sure has a way of getting me to do the right thing anyway.

Usually.

She was getting ready to say something else when Alan's shiny white Tesla turned into the driveway. I pushed my chair back, wincing as it squeaked against the old linoleum floor. Alan was one of my three favorite people on earth, but I wasn't about to get pulled into another long conversation about ethics. If we got him rolling on his skepticism bandwagon, we'd be here all night.

"Tell him hi," I said, hurrying toward the stairs. "I've got work to do."

"Okay if I tell him your plan? He'll get a kick out of it."

"Sure," I shouted as I turned the corner. No reason not to. After all, what harm could it do?

CHAPTER 10

I met Lana at our usual bench the next morning, a thick folder of flyers clamped under my arm. I'd talked her into meeting me at the butt crack of dawn, and as I walked up she was yawning in a glow of pink sunlight.

I stopped in front of her, bouncing on my toes. "Ready to get started?"

"Tell me why we needed to do this so early again?"

"Because if we move fast, we could get these all over the neighborhood before parents are leaving for work. Everyone will see them. If we get the table set up by late morning . . ." I kept bouncing. "We could make our first sale by lunch!"

She squinted at me like I was too bright for her eyes. "You stayed up all night, didn't you."

"Yep!" I answered giddily. My head felt strangely heavy and light at the same time, but it had been worth it. "It may take years of grueling work to get a degree in geophysics, but only nine hours of hyper-focused web searching are needed to become a fully certified Rock Reader."

"'Fully certified'?" she asked, raising an eyebrow. "By who?"

"By me, duh!" I said. "We're the only Rock Readers in existence. Who else would certify us?"

She groaned. "How many Dr Peppers have you had?"

I thought back, counting on my fingers. "In the last hour?"

She put her forehead in her hands. "It's going to be one of those days."

"Come on!" I said, giving her arm a tug. "If we get these flyers out, we'll have our first customer by noon."

To Lana's surprise, and mine if I'm being honest, we had our first customer even sooner.

We'd gotten back from the flyer deliveries and Lana was rearranging her rocks on the table while I decorated the sign on our easel with the most neon markers we could find.

I hadn't even heard anyone coming when suddenly a small voice behind me said, "Um, hi?"

I turned in surprise. "Mei!" I said. She was a sweet kid a couple of years younger than us who lived in Lana's neighborhood. I was used to always seeing her with her best friend, Ananya. They were inseparable, like me and Lana. It was strange seeing one of them without the other. "Are you here for a Rock Reading?"

She nodded shyly and I shifted into business mode, smooth as a river rock. "Welcome! Have a seat." I sounded confident, but inside, my heart thumped. I shared a glance with Lana. This was it: We were about to find out if I was as good a scammer as I thought.

Mei held out a couple of crumpled bills. "I only have two dollars," she said so softly I had to lean down to hear her. "I used to have more but . . ." She swallowed. "I spent it on a goodbye present for Ananya."

Lana frowned. "A goodbye present? Where'd she go?"

"Her family moved back to India," said Mei, almost in a whisper.

"Oh no!" said Lana.

I dropped my smile. "I'm so sorry." I meant it. Mei and Ananya were basically a younger version of me and Lana, and I didn't even want to imagine how I'd feel if Lana moved to another continent. "I'll tell you what. Since you're our first customer, we'll give you an eight-dollar discount."

"Really?" she asked.

"As long as it's okay with my partner?" I asked, raising my eyebrow.

"Of course," said Lana.

"Good," I said in my most authoritative voice. "Have a seat. All you have to do is pick your rock. Don't worry, you can't pick wrong. Whichever one you're drawn to, that is the right one for you." It sounded like I knew what I was talking about.

I got comfortable in my folding chair while she considered her options. Lana had spread the rocks in an organized grid on the top of the table. Mei scanned up the sedimentary row, down the igneous, and up the metamorphic. Then she passed the rows of colorful crystals and minerals. Her eyes didn't stop moving until the very last rock in the very last row. She picked it up and handed it to me. It looked like a colorful hockey puck that had been snapped in half. "This."

"Good choice. Now I consult with my partner." I turned and whispered behind my hand to Lana. "What kind of rock is this?"

"It's not actually a rock," she whispered. "It's wood. Petrified wood."

I brushed my thumb across the surface. It was as polished and smooth as glass. "No way this is wood."

"Well, not anymore," said Lana. "But it used to be. It's a slice from a tree trunk that got fossilized. When I bought it, it was a whole circle, but it broke in half by accident."

I raised my eyebrows. Of all the rocks on the table, Mei chose the one that had broken in two. This was going to be easier than I thought. But something in my gut told me I needed more.

"Okay, I need you to pick one more," I said to Mei, like that had been the plan all along.

She frowned in concentration, her eyes going up and down the rows again. This time, she stopped near the end of the fourth column and picked up a soft yellow stone that looked like a partly melted honey candy.

"Weird," said Lana. Behind her hand, she whispered, "That's not a rock either. It's amber. Fossilized tree resin. What do you think that means?"

That was the million-dollar question. Lana's job was done. It was time for me to do my thing. I closed my eyes and tuned in to my brain. To my surprise, it was spinning out so many thoughts and ideas I could barely keep up. "I've got good news," I said slowly, trying to make sense of everything in my head. I picked up the slice of wood. "You see this? This is you right now." I swear, when I said that? Tingles ran up my spine. I ignored them and kept going. "It used to be alive, just like you used to feel happy and alive, but when Ananya left, it was like part of you turned hard, like a rock. And you feel like you've been split in half, like half of you is gone forever."

Mei's eyes welled with tears. "That's exactly how I feel."

"Well, don't worry. It's going to get better. Because this?" I held up the amber. "This is your future. It's yellow, which is good, because yellow means sunshine and daisies and happy stuff like that." Ideas kept tumbling as I talked. "But that's not all. Because this is amber, or tree resin. That's like the blood of trees. Right?" I asked, turning to Lana.

"Sort of," she said. "It's the stuff that the tree secretes when it's been hurt, to heal and protect it. It clots like blood."

"Exactly!" I was so excited, I half shouted it. "That means you're protected and you're healing, and not just that, but . . ." I closed my eyes again. I pictured Mei smiling, happy, laughing with a friend. But not Ananya. I pictured someone different, someone new. "You're going to get a new best friend." I squinted at the picture in my head. "She's got kind of reddish-orange hair . . . It's amber, duh! And I think you're going to meet her near a tree, or in the forest . . ." There was an idea there, but it wasn't fully formed yet. Until suddenly, it was. "I got it! This rock is telling you to stay outside, out with the sun and the trees. Out where there's life. Because that's how you're going to find her. Stay outside, like, every day, and don't be on the lookout for someone exactly like Ananya either. This girl is going to be different, but you're going to love her."

"Wow," she said. She had lost her shyness and was leaning forward, hanging on every word. Come to think of it, so was I.

All at once, the fizzy excitement that had been building as I spoke seemed to drain out. "Okay, that's all."

She got up to leave. "Wow," she said again. "Thanks!"

I smiled weakly, trying to appear normal. "Tell people about us," I said, waving her off.

"I will!"

I waited till she couldn't see us anymore, then collapsed into my chair with a whoosh. "She sure fell for that," I said, trying to pretend like my voice wasn't shaking. "Hook, line, and sinker."

"Anyone would have fallen for that," said Lana. "It's like you weren't even you anymore. How did you do that?"

"I know, right?" I ignored her question, since I had no idea how to answer it. I kept my head down, trying not to show how dizzy I felt. "I knew I'd be good at scamming people, but I'm even better than I thought."

Lana squinted at me. "Maybe you need something to eat."

My stomach rumbled. It was true, those Dr Peppers had long since worn off.

"You stay here," she said. "I'm going to get us food from my house."

"What if someone else comes? I have no idea what any of these rocks are."

Lana puffed up with pride, then typed something into her phone. "I had a feeling we'd need this." A moment later my phone dinged. "Cheat sheet," she said proudly. "I made it last night."

"Seriously?" I opened the file she sent, and sure enough, there was my own handy guide, with a picture of each rock, its name, and a few facts next to it. Thank gourd for smart, obsessively organized friends. "You are the best of the best. I mean it. Don't you dare ever move to India. Or anywhere else, for that matter."

She patted me on my shoulder. "I'm not going anywhere." Then her face fell. "It's you we need to worry about, remember?"

Just like that, my focus came back. "I'm not going anywhere either." I scanned the park, trying to force more customers to come our way. "This business is going to fix everything. I can feel it."

CHAPTER 11

Lana dashed off to grab some snacks while I studied her cheat sheet, trying to memorize which rock was which. I wasn't expecting more customers so soon after Mei, so when I saw someone marching straight toward me from the other side of the park, I was happily surprised.

Then I realized who it was, and the flint vision came roaring back into my head, making my heart beat faster and prickles run up my spine. What was Jade Sinclair doing here? I had to remind myself that I had no reason to be scared of her.

Even if she was walking kind of aggressively.

As she got closer, her eyes skimmed over the tapestry, rock grid, and easel. And even though I knew exactly what Jade looked like, it hit me all over again how pretty she was, which was part of how she'd built such a huge following in the first place. Her legs were long, her hair was long, somehow even her neck was long. She was longer than any fourteen-year-old had any right to be.

As soon as she was close enough, she held up her phone, snapping pictures. "Scamming all the children, are we?"

Uh-oh. Aware of the phone pointed at my face, I forced myself to give her the same cheerful smile I'd give any customer. "Nope! Not a scam. Would you like a reading?"

"Yeah, no," she said lightly as she lowered her phone. "When Alan mentioned your little venture last night, I figured I'd come see for myself. And here you are, just like he said. Crystals and everything!"

A jab of annoyance distracted me from the shivers that had now reached my scalp. Why was Alan discussing me or my business with Jade?

She looked at me through long eyelashes that swept up and down. "I'm kind of a role model around here, you know? And I'm not sure I'm comfortable with all this. I feel a responsibility to my followers. I don't like the idea of someone taking advantage of them."

I held back a snort. "Good thing we're not taking advantage, then," I said brightly, refusing to break.

"Oh, please, Alan told me everything," she said, tossing a wave of hair over her shoulder.

Alan and I were going to have a talk later today. "Of course Alan assumes it's a scam," I said, thinking fast. "Skepticism is basically his religion. It would never occur to him that something like this could be true."

"Mm-hmm," she said, studying me like a specimen. "Sure."

"Fine. Stick around and judge for yourself," I said, smooth as butter. "In fact, I'm happy to give you a reading right now if you want. You can even livestream it."

A sour look flickered across her face so fast most people would've missed it. "Yeah, that's not going to happen. But I *will* be back to check on you."

"Great!" I said. "Looking forward to it."

"Toodle-oo!" she said, wiggling her fingers at me.

Toodle-whatever. That girl was toxic. How her followers didn't see right through her, I had no idea. But what was she up to, anyway? Even if Alan told her we were a scam, why would she possibly care? It made no sense.

I closed my eyes and took a deep breath to pull myself together. Jade or no Jade, I had a business to run.

CHAPTER 12

I'd been sitting at the table with my feet up for a good half hour studying Lana's cheat sheet when I finally saw someone heading my way. I squinted to see who it was.

Manuel Romero. Good. Someone I knew, and a nice guy to boot. He was in our grade, a daydreamy type who doodled nonstop through every class.

I waved him over. "Hey, Manuel. You saw our flyer?"

"Yeah," he mumbled, blushing furiously. He pulled out a bunch of wadded-up bills from his shorts pocket and dropped them on the table along with a couple of paper clips and a grubby eraser. I leaned forward, watching him pick out the money. "Eight . . . nine . . . ten." I added it to our cash box with a surge of satisfaction. It was amazing what seeing that money in the cash box did to restore my mood and spirit of professionalism. "Have a seat."

He sat with a plunk, fidgeting nervously, then glanced around. "I thought Lana was the one into rocks?"

"She is," I said, making sure to sound confident. "She'll be back soon, but don't worry, she taught me everything I need to know." Good thing Lana didn't hear me say that. But it was all made-up anyway, I reminded myself. It hardly mattered if I wasn't a rock expert.

"Pick a couple of rocks and hand them to me. I'll do the rest."

Manuel stared at the rows, considering. He reached out his hand slowly, hovered over one rock, then another, and finally picked up a dense velvety black rock called graphite. He took even longer choosing the second rock, but finally settled on the magnetite. He handed them over and said, "Is it okay if I don't have a question?"

"No problem," I said. "The rocks will guide me. Just close your eyes and clear your mind so I can tune in."

While he sat with his eyes closed, I read the notes on each rock as fast as I could. I already knew some stuff about magnetite. It was the exact rock that had given me this whole idea after Lana had put it on the table and joked that it would help us attract customers. Her notes said that it's also called lodestone, and is one of the only things on earth that is naturally magnetic. If you were a kid back in the caveman days and wanted to play with magnets, you pretty much had to go out and find yourself a couple of lodestones.

I moved on to the graphite. Graphite, it turns out, is what pencil lead is made from. Well, duh! Manuel loved to draw, and he was good at it, too. Mostly war scenes, but also tons of fantasy stuff like dragons and hobbits. I thought about the graphite and the lodestone together and smiled. This was easy. "Got it!"

Manuel opened his eyes.

"Okay, so you see this one here?" I pointed to the lodestone. "Hand me a paper clip." He picked one up from the table, wiped some fuzz off it, and dropped it in my hand. I held the lodestone over it. It stuck.

"Now watch this." I flipped to a fresh page of the pad on our easel, picked up the graphite, and ran it across the top of the page and showed him the scratchy gray line. "That rock over there is a magnet, and this one here is literally the world's oldest art tool. It's called graphite."

"Graphite," he repeated. "Cool. Can I try?"

He stood up and I handed him the chunk. He held the rock between his thumb and index finger, and moved it around the page like he'd been drawing with that exact rock his whole life. A picture formed around the line I'd drawn, which somehow now looked like the sky. Pointed hat, long black robe, black shoes, a broomstick, a cat, and a moon. "A witch!" I said, impressed. "Nice!"

He blushed, then shrugged. "Witches are cool."

"That they are," I agreed. I motioned for him to sit back down. An image had flashed through my mind as he drew and I tried to find the right words to describe what I'd seen. The vision had felt stronger than a daydream, somehow, and different too, filling my insides with a strange quivery fizziness. "So there's something you want, like really bad, something that's attracting you like a magnet. It either has to do with drawing, or you're going to use your drawing to get it. In my vision, I saw you at a table doing some art, and I just *knew* it was going to happen..." I stopped. The feeling had felt so real, but now it was vague, like trying to remember a dream. I wished I had something more specific to say. "It has to do with art," I finished lamely.

But instead of asking for his money back, Manuel's eyes went wide. "Art school. That's exactly what I was going to ask you about. There's this boarding school—I really want to go but it's crazy expensive." He slumped a little. "It'll never happen."

I stared at him, chills running up and down my arms as the fizzy feeling started fizzing again. "That's it! That's definitely it. What do you have to do to get in?"

"I need a portfolio, references, tons of stuff. It'll take months to put it all together."

"So do it," I said. "Start today. Like, right now."

He hesitated, then deflated again. "My parents . . . They can't . . . Scholarships are almost impossible to get. Seriously, I have no shot."

"Look, you're going. Trust me. I'm not sure how, exactly, but . . . just get started on the portfolio, okay? Take that witch for starters, she's awesome."

Manuel nodded with his lips pressed together. We'd never talked like this before. It felt nice being the person he opened up to. What was weird is that even though I was making the whole thing up, it didn't feel scammy at all.

He stood, then pointed to his drawing with his thumb. "Keep it. She's yours."

"Thanks!" I said. That's when I noticed her hair. Chin-length curls, like mine, and a round face like mine, too. Huh.

After he walked away, I flipped the page back so our sign was showing, but I liked knowing the witch was underneath it, like a secret. When I turned around Lana was standing there, a sweaty silver thermos in each hand with plastic bags of snacks hanging off her pinkies, her gray backpack straining under the weight of rocks. "I heard that," she said, giving me the old hairy eyeball. "It was impressive. Like, weirdly impressive. Again. You sound like a real psychic."

"I'm just a very good scammer," I said. "As we both know."

Her eyebrow stayed arched. "I'm not kidding. It's spooky. How are you doing it?"

It was clear she wanted to talk about it, but I did not. So instead I laughed, making my voice go deep like a voice-over on a movie trailer. "The secrets of the Superior Scam Artist must never be revealed."

She gave in, knowing it was no use trying to get anything out of me I didn't want to give. "Fine. Ready for a break, Superior Scam Artist?" She held up the drinks.

I realized how completely beat I felt. "I don't suppose one of those thermoses has caffeine in it?"

"Iced tea it is," she said, handing me the thermos in her right hand. "The other one is lemonade. Sorry it took so long. I wanted to make sure I had the right rocks."

I took a long swallow of the cool sweet tea, then let out a long, satisfied sigh. "All is forgiven. You are my actual savior, and not just because of the drinks. That cheat sheet was perfect. Not nearly as good as having you here, though," I added quickly. Then I made a face. "By the way, you'll never guess who else came by while you were gone. Jade Sinclair."

"What? Why?" She got momentarily hopeful. "I don't suppose she wanted a reading?"

"I wish." I gave her the full play-by-play, which made her shake her head.

"Ugh," she said when I finished. "She's horrible. Why does she even care what we're doing?"

"That's what I want to know."

"Maybe she's bored?" asked Lana. "Or looking for drama. It's probably hard finding things to post about all the time."

From there, we fell into the same conversation we'd had a million times before about how glad we were we didn't really do much social media.

And that, by the way, is exactly how to tell your best friends apart from the rest. Your best friends are the ones you can have the same conversation with over and over again, and somehow it never feels boring or old. Instead, it just gets cozier and more comfortable, like sleeping in your dad's old flannel sheets.

"Anyway," I said, "if Alan stays with Jade's mother, Jade is going to eat him alive." As I said it, the picture of the flint leapt back into my mind, along with the sparks of fire.

Lana tugged on her braid. "Do you think Jade will mess things up for us?"

"No way. We're going to make this work no matter what."

CHAPTER 13

Unfortunately, we had more caffeinated drinks than customers the rest of that day. Luckily the park had a porta-potty. Between bathroom breaks and very few customers, it was mostly just a bunch of hot, boring waiting.

"Forty-two dollars isn't half bad for our first day," said Lana as she packed up her rocks.

"Minus the ten dollars we owe my mom for the paper," I grumbled. "I wonder why that woo-woo Feather kid never showed up. If we can get her to hang a flyer in her store, we'll get more customers for sure."

"Hopefully she'll come tomorrow," said Lana. "She seemed excited enough."

I bit my lip. "Do you think I'm good enough to fool her?"

"You're good enough to fool anyone," she said. "For real. It's spooky."

"You keep saying that. But you're dealing with a Superior Scam Artist, remember?"

"Uh-huh," she said vaguely, picking up her overstuffed backpack and squinting at me.

"Oh just stop," I said, giving her the biggest eye roll possible. I could see what she was thinking and wanted to nip it right in the bud. "Don't you dare go all woo-woo magic on me. That is the absolute *last* thing I need."

She laughed. "Fine. But if you don't want me turning all woo, maybe don't be so good at it tomorrow."

I gave her a big grin. "Deal."

By the time I walked through my front door, the exhaustion seemed to catch up with me at once. I dragged myself into the kitchen and collapsed into a chair at the table.

"Hey, Sewer Rat." My mom's top half was deep in the fridge, rummaging through the vegetable bin. When she stood up, she was holding a bunch of deformed-looking carrots and cucumbers. "Whoa. Are you okay?"

"I'm fine," I mumbled. "What's with the ugly veggies?"

"Turns out you can get ugly veggies on the cheap," she said, sounding artificially bright. "They're just as nutritious as the pretty ones. And no offense, but you look worse than the carrots right now." She pressed her palm gently to my forehead. "What's up?"

"Just hot," I said, putting my head down to rest against the cool, smooth surface of the table. "Maybe a little tired."

The ice machine grinded as ice clinked into a glass. "Raspberry seltzer?"

"Mmmmm," I said gratefully as she poured the sparkling drink. My mom might have enough piercings to set off airport metal detectors, but she's a real mom where it counts.

"You're not just a little tired, you're exhausted." She set the glass on the table in front of me and smoothed a strand of blue hair behind her ear. "The question is, are you good exhausted, or bad exhausted?"

"Good, I think. We made semi-decent money for the first day."

She dumped the malformed veggies into a colander and put it in the sink. She glanced at me sideways. "So you're going to keep doing it?"

"Of course! Why wouldn't I?"

She rolled her eyes. "Oh, gee, I don't know. Maybe because it's making you sick? Or maybe you're feeling sick because secretly, deep inside, you're just a little bit guilty?"

I put my head back on the table and closed my eyes. Not that again. And even if I did feel guilty at first, I didn't anymore. My readings might be total bullstink, but they were helping people. Like our first customer, Mei. That girl was bound to make a new friend. I just sped the process along by telling her to stay outside. If I hadn't, she might have stayed locked up inside all summer staring at her phone, which is a great way to never make a friend.

And what about this kid named Josh who'd come later in the day. He limped up to the stand, his ankle wrapped, and picked a chunk of pinkish rock salt. I remembered that once, when I twisted my elbow, my mom had me soak it in a sink full of salt water. Somehow, I knew with 100 percent certainty that if Josh did the same, he'd heal up in no time. Did I help that kid? No question. Did he get his money's worth? Heck yeah!

Not that I could explain any of this to my mom, at least not without sounding like a total dung hump. I forced myself out of my chair and grabbed a wooden cutting board. "I didn't sleep last night, that's all. I'll be fine tomorrow. Hey!" I added, picking up a cucumber. "By the way, wait till you hear what Alan did."

She glanced over her shoulder, a dripping dish suspended over the sink. "What?"

I made a face. "He told Jade Sinclair about the Rock Reading."

"He told Jade? Huh. But . . . is that bad? I mean, don't you want people to know?"

"Yes, but he also told her it's a scam," I said. "She stopped by today and was all threatening, like 'I know what you're up to and I won't let you get away with it.'"

My mom turned fully around, still holding the plate, getting drips on the old linoleum floor. "Seriously?"

"Yeah," I said, "she started claiming she has a 'responsibility to her followers.'" I put my fingers in air quotes and huffed in disgust. "Instead of being a huge source of customers, Jade wants to tank us."

The more I talked about it the more worked up I got. And poor Alan. He wins the Worst Timing Ever Award because I'd reached peak wrath when his white Tesla pulled into the garage.

I didn't even give him a chance to say hello. "Why did you tell Jade Sinclair about the Rock Reading?"

He froze, then tilted his head. "But . . . but it wasn't a secret. Your flyers are everywhere. I was trying to help! I figured who could spread the word better than Jade?"

"But you told her I'm a con artist!"

He held up his hands. "Whoa, I did no such thing. I swear it. I mentioned your business, but not the scam part. Unless . . ." He let his laptop bag fall slowly to the floor beside him. "She must have heard me talking to Brandy."

"You told Jade's mom I'm a scammer?"

"What? No! I was telling her about the video of your dad I just found, and what he said, and how it inspired you. Jade wasn't even in the room."

"So she was eavesdropping on you. And now she wants to tank us."

"I'm really sorry, Geo. I had no idea." His face got so tragic it was almost comical. "What can I do?"

How could I stay angry at Alan? It really wasn't his fault.

"It's fine," I said, sighing. "Don't worry about it."

"Well, I'm going to talk to her for sure," he said determinedly.

"No way. Don't say a word. We're already on her radar enough as it is."

"But she needs to be told it's not okay."

Alan meant well, but the absolute last thing I needed was someone disciplining Jade on my behalf. "Seriously, *please*—"

But he cut me off with a shake of his head. "Her mother needs to know, and Jade needs a proper consequence."

"Mom?" I asked, begging her to see my side.

"Alan—" she started, then sighed. She turned to me instead. "She does need consequences, and I'm sure Alan will handle it carefully."

I slumped helplessly back in my chair. There would be consequences, all right. Consequences for me.

CHAPTER 14

Lana and I were setting up shop the next morning after another sugar bomb breakfast when I heard a fake-friendly voice calling from behind. "Well, hello again!"

"Oh boy," said Lana, looking up.

Oh boy was right. Jade had come even sooner than I'd expected, and this time she had a bunch of her followers in tow, their phones recording my every move.

Well, whatever she had planned for me, I wasn't going to make it easy. I forced my shoulders to relax, then swept my eyes across the group of them with my most professional smile. "Welcome to the Rock Readers. What can we do for you?"

Jade smiled back, sat herself down at the rock table, and held out a ten-dollar bill so fresh and crisp it looked ironed.

I blinked. "You want a reading?"

"You're the psychic, you tell me." She narrowed her eyes. "You clearly like telling people things." I stared at the money like it was a snake. She was up to something, no question about it. My mind raced, trying to find the trap, while I sat there saying nothing like an idiot.

"See?" She whipped the ten dollars back, then turned to the raised phones. "She can't do it. Because she's not a real psychic."

She lowered her giant sunglasses so she was looking her viewers right in the eye. "This so-called Rock Reader is a scammer. She's taking money off little kids, and we're going to stop her."

"That's not true," I said, trying to keep my footing. I turned to one of the phones. "We're the real deal, worth every penny. Just keep watching and I'll prove it."

"Fine. Go ahead and tell me my 'fortune' and we'll see how good you are. Just remember, we're live streaming on four different platforms."

"Perfect," I said, doing my best to seem unfazed. "But I'll need that ten dollars back." Her nostrils flared ever so slightly as she held it out. I yanked it away and passed it to Lana, who put it in the cash box.

"Now," I continued, "pick two rocks."

Jade hesitated, then barely glanced at the table before grabbing the first rock she saw.

The flint.

Just for a moment, I couldn't speak. My throat went dry as the vision of flames roared back through my head.

I snuffed it out, quick, with a small cough. "Okay, now one more."

Behind her sunglasses, her eyes rolled. "Like it matters." But she glanced down again, actually looking at the rocks this time, and chose a rough green chunk from the middle of the table. It was a strange choice. If she liked green, she could have gone for the bold, bright malachite, or the soft, pretty aventurine. This was a dark and ugly green, like limp seaweed or slimy mold, or the color you turn just before you barf. Maybe picking such a plain, ugly rock was an attempt to throw me, but I still preferred it to the sharp, fiery flint.

"An interesting choice," I said, dropping the flint like a hot potato and focusing all my attention on the ugly rock instead. I leaned back and whispered to Lana. "I remember the flint, but what's this one called again?"

Jade must have had ears like a bat, because she snorted with delight. "Did you hear that?" she said to the cameras. "She has no idea what these rocks are!"

"Hey," I said sharply. "Lana's the rock expert, I'm the psychic. Consulting with her is exactly how this works."

I leaned back toward Lana. "Lizardite," she whispered even more quietly. "A kind of serpentine."

Lizards and serpents? Seriously?

"They call it that because it reminds people of reptile skin," she continued. "And it feels almost greasy and slick if you cut it. Also, it gets inside other rocks and, it's hard to explain, but it kind of takes over. Some people even call it a zombie rock."

Lizards, serpents, and now zombies? It was probably just my imagination, but the rock suddenly felt slippery in my hand. Much as I thought a slithery rock suited Jade perfectly, I needed to tell her something positive or I'd scare her viewers away. "Can you tell me anything about it that's *not* super creepy?" I whisper-asked Lana.

"It's the official state rock of California? At least, serpentine is, so that kind of counts? Also, when you polish it . . ." She glanced across the table and blinked.

"What?"

"It looks like jade. The gemstone. Sometimes people polish it and sell it as jade, as a scam."

Whoa.

"Excuse me," interrupted Jade. "Is this all you plan to do? Whisper?"

"Do you want a reading or not?" I snapped. Jade had no response, which made me feel the teensiest bit smug. Then I saw Feather coming toward our table.

My stomach tightened. Faking out all of Jade's dimwitted internet followers was one thing. Doing it in front of them *and* a kid who worked in an actual New Age shop was another. She might be able to tell the difference between me and the real deal. And if she said anything to expose me, even without meaning to, I'd be humiliated in real time for all to see.

Jade caught my hesitation and pounced. "Why, hello!" she said, turning her entire body toward Feather. "And who might you be?" All the cameras swerved. If it were possible for someone to dissolve into liquid and seep into the ground, Feather surely would have. She opened her mouth, said, "um," then closed it.

It was Lana who saved her. "This is Feather," she said. "She's here visiting her aunt."

Jade laughed like this was too good to be true. "Did you say *Feather*?"

"Hey. Don't make fun of people's names," I said coolly. "It's mean."

Jade shot me a nasty look as the phones swiveled back toward me. As soon as she wasn't in the spotlight anymore, Feather found her voice, even if it was more of a breathless squeak. "Um, I'm so sorry I couldn't come yesterday. Do you mind if I watch?"

"Please do!" said Jade, seeming to understand the entire situation in an instant. "In fact, here, you can sit with me." She scooched over and patted the empty half of her seat.

"Um, thanks?" squeaked Feather, who looked like she wished she'd never come. She perched tentatively on the chair, ready to jump at a moment's notice. Jade, who looked like a hawk hanging out with the mouse she was saving for dinner, turned back to me with predatory glee. "You were about to say?"

I looked from Jade to Feather, my lips pressed together. Trying to fool one while outwitting the other was going to stretch my smarts to their absolute limit, but there was nothing to do but plunge ahead. With the slimy lizardite still in my hand, I closed my eyes, took a deep breath, and thought through everything Lana had told me about the rock. The only problem was that the more I thought, the creepier the whole thing started to feel. Not only was the rock named after lizards and snakes, but it was a zombie rock, and sold as fake jade to boot. I was overcome with a strong urge to chuck it across the playground and wash my hands. Instead, I refocused on the only good thing about it: the color green. Not the nasty dark shade of the rock, but a nicer kind of green. The color of plants and spring. New life. Growth. That was better. I could work with that.

Besides, I reminded myself, I'm making it all up anyway. What did it matter what I said? Dropping the lizardite back onto the table and giving my hands a quick wipe on my shorts, I said, "That's lizardite, and it's the perfect rock for you, because it's the closest thing to actual jade that we've got on the table. It doesn't look like jade right now, but it would if you cut and polished it. And it's green like jade, which stands for growing. So, for starters, you're going to get even taller than you already are. You might even get Lana-tall, which is great . . ."

I opened my hands like I was presenting Lana. "Because as you can see, Lana-tall is awesome."

Lana blushed, but Jade just snorted with delight. "A growth spurt? That's your big prediction?"

I cleared my throat. "I'm not finished. The *point* is that you're growing, but not just in height. Because you know what else green represents? New beginnings. Rebirth. Change."

I paused, distracted by the feeling growing in my gut. Somehow, I was pretty sure I was right about an upcoming change, but it was a slimy, slithery kind of transformation, not the good kind of change.

"Change? *New beginnings?* Yeah, because that's not vague or anything." She rolled her eyes at Feather like they were old friends in on a joke. "Anyone who falls for this garbage deserves to be scammed, agreed? I think my work here is done."

Feather, to her credit, didn't nod or smile back. If anything, she frowned and leaned away like she'd smelled something bad.

"Stop interrupting," I said, my teeth on edge. "I'm still not finished. I didn't even get to the other rock yet."

"Oh, I think we're good. This was perfect. Even lamer than I expected." She turned toward the cameras with a smirk. "Like I said, she's nothing but a scam artist. Stay away from this fake 'psychic'!"

That was it. Cameras or no cameras, scary Jade or no scary Jade, I no longer cared. I opened the cash box and took out her bill. "Money-back guarantee. Here you go." I flicked it at her. Then I turned and stared at the cameras. "Lana and I are the real deal, and I'm happy to prove it to each and every one of you, if you promise to actually sit and let me finish the reading. If you think I'm a fake, you'll get your money back, and that's a promise. We're in the park by the yellow stegosaurus every day from eight a.m. to—"

Jade lurched to her feet. "Don't fall for it. She's scamming you!"

All at once an image burst into my mind, sharp and bright. The image was my foot slamming into Jade's skinny butt, booting her clear across the sky like a scene from a cartoon. I saw her flying through the air getting farther and farther, tinier and tinier, until she was flying over a map of the United States like a little bug. She landed with a poof somewhere deep in the middle of a forest in California, and suddenly, with an explosion of chills, I just knew.

"Jade Sinclair is moving to California," I announced, standing up so fast my chair fell backward. "And soon, too." I whirled around to face her head-on. "*That's* the reading. Specific enough for you?"

I could tell by the fire shooting out her eyes that she wanted to put her hands around my neck and squeeze. Instead, she flicked a long wave of tousled hair behind her shoulder and pretended to laugh. "Okay. Sure thing. Like *that's* ever going to happen."

"Adios!" I shouted as she stalked off, her entourage in tow. "Hope it happens soon!"

Once they were gone, I picked my chair up off the ground and collapsed into it, mortified to feel tears prickling the backs of my eyes.

"That was . . ." started Lana. She ended with a wide-eyed shake of her head.

In the silence that followed, Feather cleared her throat. "I don't suppose you still have that sage?"

CHAPTER 15

Turns out, we did still have the sage. Lana had tucked it in her backpack for safekeeping, along with a pack of matches. Feather removed it with reverence and I learned that if you are woo-woo you believe that lighting a bunch of stinky herbs on fire then waving the smoke all over the place clears the negative energy left behind by toxic people. Or some stupid junk like that. So I basically sat there forcing a Serious and Respectful Face while Feather literally blew smoke up my butt.

"Woo boy," she said as she waved. "That girl had some serious bad energy. Like, serious. I lived in California for almost a year and my school was filled with toxic people. But that girl? She's not just a regular mean girl. She's . . ."

"Evil," I finished. Despite the sweat pouring off me, chills rippled over my arms. That's exactly what I'd been thinking about Jade.

"I hate to say that about anyone, right? But with her, I felt it the second my hip touched hers on that chair. Something is really off with her." She shook her head and kept sage-ing, or smoodging, or whatever. She did the whole table, each individual rock, and then even made a big smoke ring around Steggy for good measure. When she was done the entire playground was hanging with haze and a strong smell of burning herbs.

I wrinkled my nose. "People are definitely going to think we're doing drugs."

"Sorry," said Feather. "I wanted to be thorough."

"Oh, you were thorough all right." I coughed. "I can't sense her anywhere."

Feather nodded, satisfied. "Good. It will help draw more people to your stand, too. Better people." She smashed the end of the stick into some damp mulch until it stopped smoking, then handed it to Lana, who placed it carefully back into the lockbox. You never know when you might need another smoke-fest, I guess.

Her job done, Feather reverted to awkwardness. After rubbing her arms for a while, she worked up some nerve and sputtered, "Um, I was wondering . . . I mean, it's fine if you're too drained, I wouldn't blame you obviously, but if you're not feeling too bad and . . . um . . ."

She was blushing hard and saying more ums than a nervous Alan. Lana put her out of her misery. "We'd love to give you a reading. Right, Geo?"

"Of course." I coughed and added, "All that smoke perked me right up."

She dropped down across from me with a whoosh. "Thank you!" Then she opened up a homemade-looking tote bag of stitched-together patchwork cloth and began rummaging.

"Hey, don't worry about the money," I said. "Yours is free . . . if you could put some flyers in your aunt's shop?"

"Really?" she gushed. "Of course! That's so nice!"

There was nothing nice about it. It was a smart marketing move, pure and simple. I had a weird, sudden urge to warn Feather about me. I didn't mind faking everyone else out, but she was just so . . .

From out of nowhere, a picture flashed through my head. A picture of her, me, and Lana. But she hadn't even picked her rocks yet, and, in any case, I wasn't sure I liked what I'd seen.

"Go ahead and choose," I said, trying to clear my head.

Her eyes ran up and down the rows. Hesitantly, she reached out for one, then another rock, and handed them to me.

"Moonstone and smoky quartz," said Lana.

It was an interesting pair. Both looked like something magical and ethereal trapped in solid form: the moonstone like solidified moonbeams, the smoky quartz like a chunk of smoke and mist. Somehow, I didn't even need Lana to tell me more about them. I knew just what to say.

"You are an extremely sensitive person," I said, starting with the obvious. "You're, like, super . . ." I searched for the right word. Magical? That was close. "Mystical," I finished, cringing internally. Super mystical? What a cheesy thing to say. If some psychic had told me that, I would have rolled my eyes and snorted. But Feather beamed, so I plunged forward.

"The problem is that you're not just, like, emotionally sensitive. There are physical things, too, things that are fine for most people, that aren't good for you. Like . . ." I thought about all the smoke in the quartz and the answer came quick. "Pollution." Then I thought of moonbeams streaming through a clear night sky and added, "Sunlight, too. Most people love sun, but it isn't good for you."

I had gone out on a limb, but it paid off. Feather was nodding vigorously. "That's exactly right! It's one of the reasons I hated California. When the sun hits me, I get nauseous and weak all over. I was scared to come here in the summer because it's so hot, but at least here you have plenty of shade."

"Yeah." I nodded, as if I knew all about it. "You'd do better somewhere cool and misty, like Seattle or Scotland."

"Oh, I just *adore* Scotland!" she gushed. "It's my soul home."

I closed my eyes again, partly to keep my face straight. "But it's more than just the weather. Any kind of harsh thing is bad for you. Vaping, drugs, alcohol, all that stuff. Social media, too. Definitely stay away from that."

"Yes! I *despise* social media!" she said, her enthusiasm so high I could practically see the exclamation points hovering in the air above her.

"Right. Some kids love that kind of thing, but it would wreck you. Stay away from all that stuff. Harsh people especially."

People like me.

My eyes popped open. Where had all that come from? And why was fizz frothing in my gut again?

Feather was eating it up. "You're right. Of course you are. It's not exactly easy, though."

"That's the real reason you came here," I said, knowing all at once that it was 100 percent true. "To get away from toxic kids."

Feather's eyes filled with tears. "They were horrible."

Lana reached out and squeezed her arm. "You'll like it here. Not everyone is like Jade. There're lots of nice kids."

Suddenly, my mind was filled with the same picture that had started to form earlier, the one I had batted away, and with it came fresh ripples of fizz. It was me, Lana, and Feather, sitting in a circle on a polished wood floor, laughing like crazy together. I only saw it for a second, but it was so real I could still feel the coolness of the floor under my legs. Where were we? It for sure wasn't my room or Lana's room. Did Feather have wood floors in hers?

No. I didn't want to know. There was absolutely no way I was going to end up friends with this insecure woo-woo hippie girl. I didn't care how nice she was. If anything, I was exactly the kind of harsh person I had just told her to avoid. Wasn't I?

"Are you getting something else?" she asked, staring at me with big eyes. "I felt your energy shift."

I opened my mouth, then closed it. I didn't want to tell her what I'd seen, but I had to tell her something. And obviously she needed friends. So I told her exactly what I'd told Mei. "Er . . . try to stay outside this summer as much as possible. You'll find nice friends that way."

Her nose crinkled. "But I'm supposed to avoid the sun, remember? Because too much sun is bad for me?"

Ugh, dang it, how had I messed that up? *Think, brain, think!* "Um, um . . . umbrella!" I blurted. "Yes. I'm seeing one right now. Huge. Purple. Plenty of shade under that thing. So, er . . . yeah. Just find one of those, then you can stay outside as long as you want. That's how you'll get friends." My stomach churned. Even though lying to people was the whole point of the scam, this was the first time one of my readings actually *felt* like a scam. And it felt terrible. Worse, if she took my advice, she was going to look like a major ding-brain. Carrying around a giant sun-umbrella was definitely not going to make it easier for her to find friends. But it was too late to take it back now.

Lana was staring daggers at me, but when she shifted her eyes to Feather, they turned soft and kind. "I'm pretty sure I can find an umbrella exactly like that at home. I could get it for you if you want? Then you could stay here and hang out with us."

Whoa! Wait! What? That was *not* what I had meant. I had meant hang out outside *somewhere else*. Not with us. But Feather was squealing and gushing, "I'd love that! Thank you!"

I was trying to signal a "stop!" warning to Lana while at the same time act fake-pleased at Feather's happiness, which was only resulting in making me look constipated. Luckily, something distracted us. Lana poked me in the shoulder. "Geo. Check it out!"

Feather squealed again. "The sage worked. It's drawing customers!"

I knew it was Jade's free video advertising, not the sage, but sure enough three kids were walking toward us across the grass. The thought of doing more readings made me want to collapse, but these weren't just clients, I reminded myself. They were ten-dollar bills.

So I stood up and gave my new customers a big, confident smile. "Welcome to our Rock Reading table. The line forms next to the dinosaur."

CHAPTER 16

We had pretty good business the rest of that day. This made me happy for two reasons: 1) the money, and 2) knowing Jade's sabotage attempt had backfired completely. *Ha!*

Even though it was obviously the social media exposure that was boosting our business, I made sure to give credit to Feather and the burning stink-stick she'd waved around. It made her so happy thinking she'd helped. She beamed as she sat under the shade of the enormous, ridiculous purple golf umbrella Lana had dug out from a pile somewhere deep in her house.

As the day went on, I realized something: If I let my subconscious form images in my mind and simply told my customers what I was seeing, I ended up with that fizzy feeling, which was pretty nice as long as I didn't fight it too hard. When I ignored the images, or made something random up, my stomach would clench and I'd feel sick. I tried not to think about what that meant. Either way, it was tiring work.

At the end of the day I stumbled back to my house, still pretending there weren't a million and a half questions banging around my brain. Questions like, what the heck were these pictures forming in my head? Where were they coming from? And *how*? But since I couldn't begin to answer them, instead I focused on worrying about real things. Like Jade. Why hadn't we heard from her since that morning? She hadn't even posted anything else. But something told me she wasn't about to back down and disappear from my life, as much as I wish she would.

My mom solved the mystery while we fixed some beans and rice for dinner. "It's just you and me for the next few nights. Alan surprised Jade and her mom with a last-minute trip to the beach, no phones allowed."

"Ahh," I said, shaking beans out of the can. "That explains it." Suddenly, I turned. "Hold on . . . you don't mean California, do you?"

"No," she said with a question on her face. "Why on earth would they go to California when we have a perfectly nice beach two hours from here?"

"Never mind," I said, quickly turning the empty can right side up before I dripped bean juice all over the place. Muscles I hadn't even known were tense began to relax. It was going to be wonderful to have three days of not worrying about Jade.

I got to the playground bright and early the next day and found Lana already setting up. "Hey," she said, placing a shimmery selenite wand carefully between a striped tiger's eye and thin sliver of mica that sparkled when the sun hit it. "How are you feeling?"

"Much better," I said. "With luck we'll get more customers than ever."

She paused, a smooth, sharp piece of obsidian in her hand. "I'm not sure more customers would be good for you. You seemed almost sick by the end yesterday."

I crossed my arms. "Of course I can handle more customers. It was the heat, that's all."

"I don't think it was the heat. It was . . . intense." She put down the obsidian and stood up, tossing her braid back over her shoulder. "When you give a reading, it's like . . . the energy changes."

I waved my fingers in the air. "Okay, Feather."

"Maybe I do sound like her," she pushed on. "But seriously, all that stuff you say, where does it come from?"

I pointed to my temple. "Gray matter. I'm filled with it."

She huffed. "It isn't just a bunch of BS. I'm not buying it."

I sighed. "Please don't get all spooky on me, Lana. You're too smart for that. If you keep going on like this, I'm going to have to sic Alan on you. He'll talk some good, skeptical sense back into you."

Lana pressed her lips together. Before we could say more, we noticed a girl with a fierce-looking buzz cut running toward us from the far side of the park.

I grabbed Lana's arm. "Oh my gourd. It's a Jackson sister." There were no fewer than eight Jackson sisters, each one more athletic than the last, and most wearing buzz cuts. If I shaved off my hair I'd look like I had a giant wad of raw dough slapped on top of my neck. But when a Jackson sister does it, it looks edgy and fierce and intimidatingly cool. Basically, if I made a social status pyramid for every grade, there'd be a Jackson sister pegged at the top spot of each and every one. Not only that, but they babysat just about everyone. If one of them liked our reading, we'd be neck-deep in customers all summer long.

As she got closer, I saw it was Zafirah Jackson, who was already in high school. She ran all the way to the card table and came to a skidding stop. "I can't believe I'm doing this," she panted, her eyes wild. "But I'm desperate. Harold is gone. I've got to find him quick!"

"Harold?" I wrinkled my brow. "Is that your dog?"

"No!" she said, bouncing from foot to foot. "My snake."

"A snake," I said, processing. "Okaaay. Go ahead and sit down. You need to pick some rocks first."

She barely glanced at the table before waving it off. "Can we skip that part? I don't want my fortune told. I just need you to tell me where he is."

Lana gasped. "Skip the rocks?"

"Sorry. It's just that he's the only thing in my house that is completely mine, and if one of my sisters finds him first, he's dead. Literally. That was the agreement. If one of them finds him out of his cage, even once . . ." She slid her finger across her throat.

"Okay." I nodded, understanding the rush. "Got it. But we're Rock Readers. We can't do it without the rocks. Just pick two fast and I'll tune in quick as I can."

She didn't even sit down. She plucked the two closest to her and tossed them at me one after the other. "Bentonite, fluorite," announced Lana as they sailed through the air.

I caught them, stared at them dumbly for a few seconds, then promptly panicked. My customers weren't supposed to demand specific things like the exact location of some slithering creature. How was I supposed to fake that? And even if I did somehow know where he was, nothing was keeping him from wriggling off to some other creepy place. He could be long gone already.

"Okay," I blustered. "I'm getting something, but I need to confer with my partner before I'm sure." I did my best to maintain professional dignity while grabbing Lana's arm and pulling her behind Steggy.

"I told you none of this is real," I hissed. "I have no idea what to say. I'm drawing a massive blank!"

Her eyes went big. "What are you going to do?"

"I have to think of something. Tell me more about the rocks."

"Bentonite is a clay. See how it's all powdery and soft? It's used in all kinds of ways. Manufacturing, industry. Some people say it's purifying. Remember that time we tried face masks?"

I remembered all right. Our faces had been covered in nasty, thick paste, which struck me as gross at the time and even more so now. "That was this stuff?" I asked. Lana nodded.

"It swells when wet, too. That's why it's a main ingredient in kitty litter."

"We put *kitty litter* on our faces?" I shook my head to clear it. "Never mind, don't answer that. What about the other rock?" This one was hard and translucent, a pretty blue-green color with swirls of purple.

"Fluorite," she said.

"Fluoride?" I said. "Like toothpaste?"

She shook her head, then nodded. "No, it's fluor-*ite*, not fluor-*ide*. But you're right, kind of, because fluoride comes from fluorite. It's also used to make lenses for glasses."

A tingle went up my back, something flashed on the movie screen of my mind. Something white in a dark place, and suddenly, I knew. "Got it!" I said. I skidded back to the table where Zafirah was eyeing me with vague distrust.

"You have cats, yes?" I asked.

Zafirah nodded. "Three."

"Okay, where do you keep the litter box?"

"We have one downstairs in the laundry room, one in the upstairs bathroom."

Bingo. "Harold is in the bathroom."

"But I already checked the bathrooms," she said. "I looked *everywhere*."

"Look again," I said. "Trust me. Look under the sinks, behind the toilets, even down the drains, but check especially good behind the litter box. And if you have a toothpaste drawer, check that too—in, under, behind, around. And do it quick before he slithers somewhere else!"

She nodded, her eyes blazing with purpose and hope, then ran.

"Wait!" I yelled after her. "What about the ten dollars?"

"Sorry," she shouted over her shoulder. "I'll pay you later."

"Later?" No way. I had a better idea. Zafirah had gotten far enough away that I had to shout with my hands cupped around my mouth. "I'll make it free if you promise to tell everyone about us."

She gave me a thumbs-up as she dashed across the street and disappeared from view.

"Hmph," I said, crossing my arms. "She'd better stick to the deal."

But Lana was staring at me. "You know exactly where that snake is, don't you?"

The feeling of *knowing* shivered through me again and with it came a fresh surge of fizz. I slammed it into an imaginary lockbox and turned the key. "Of course not. How could I?"

She gave me a look of Lana-stubbornness.

"Oh, come on. I have to sound like I believe it, otherwise they won't believe it either. Sounding cocky is ninety percent of the con."

"If you were making up where Zafirah's snake is just now, that's a huge risk."

"Nah. It's a calculated risk. If the snake happens to be in the bathroom, we win BIG."

"And if he's not?"

I shrugged. "That just means he slithered away before Zafirah got to him. It wouldn't mean I was wrong. And she can't complain since she didn't even pay, right?"

"Hmm," Lana said, crossing her arms.

"Look, here comes someone else," I said, happy to change the subject. We squinted into the sun. "Oh no," I groaned. "Not Cassie Breadman."

CHAPTER 17

Lana saw Cassie slump-walking toward us and whispered, "Good luck with this one."

Cassie was in our grade. She was about as opposite from a Jackson sister as you could ever get. Pale instead of dark, slack instead of strong, needy instead of self-assured, and whiny instead of fun. Top that off with a tendency toward stalking, and you can guess why I was not super thrilled to see her.

"At least you can predict what she's going to ask," Lana added with a grin. She could say that again. Any kid who talked to her for more than five seconds could predict what she'd ask. Cassie Breadman was completely love obsessed. She'd been nursing an unhealthy crush on the same wildly disinterested kid since kindergarten. She was going to ask one thing and one thing only: Did William Frank love her back?

This posed a big problem for me, because absolutely anyone except poor Cassie herself could tell you that William Frank did not love her back and never would. And she was not going to like hearing that.

So I made sure to wait until Lana had safely locked her ten-dollar bill in the box before beginning. One she'd settled into the chair, I explained how it worked and waited as she slowly scanned the rows of rocks, then, in a shock to no one, selected the heart-shaped rose quartz and another pink rock that looked like it was covered in glitter.

But I already knew it didn't matter which rocks she picked. So I made a decision, set both rocks aside, and focused on her, instead.

"Cass, I don't want to hear it. You're obsessed. It's not healthy."

She blushed. "You have no idea what I was going to ask—"

"Come on. My dead grandmother knows what you're going to ask. My dead grandmother's dead mail carrier knows."

Her eyes went huge. "Can you talk to dead people?"

"Ugh, no! What I'm trying to say is that everyone knows you're obsessed. You've got to give him up. I'm sorry to tell you this, but it's never going to work. Like, ever. Put on some Taylor Swift and get over it."

She pursed her lips.

"Look, Cass, it's nothing personal. It's not about you. It's just that William is one hundred percent a gamer, right? He doesn't care about girls. Not yet, anyway. Maybe when he's older, but not now."

Somehow, Cassie took this as meaning that she just had to wait a bit. "He turns fourteen on October third. I'm getting him a Minecraft sword and a trunk filled with—"

"Cass, NO. No! No sword, no trunk, no nothing. Didn't you hear me? You need to calm down. Let the guy breathe for a while without panting at him."

She deflated. "But I already started the origami creepers—"

I cut her off. "You came here for the truth, right?"

She stuck out her lower lip, but eventually she gave a teeny nod.

"Good. Because you need to focus on yourself. Figure out what *you* like."

"But William—"

"No! Not William. YOU. If you like Minecraft for real, that's fine. Then go do Minecraft. But don't do it for some boy, okay? And if you like something else, then do that thing instead. He'll respect you for it, I promise."

"And that will make him like me?"

I smacked my head. "Oh my gourd! Seriously! Cut him out of your thoughts for at least a year. Okay? I mean it."

"A year?!"

I stared at her until she seemed to melt into her chair a little bit. "Can I have my ten dollars back?" she asked in a whiny voice.

"Definitely," I said. "And I'll tell you what. Instead of a Rock Reading, I'll make you a deal: If you can go one year without saying his name, even once, come back and I'll give you fifty dollars plus a real reading, rocks and everything. Strictly honor code. How's that?"

"Fifty dollars? Really?" For the first time I saw the spark of something besides William Frank in her eye.

I thrust out my hand. "Meet me here one year from now. Promise?"

She looked skeptical, but she shook on it. As she slinked away a feeling of sweet satisfaction ran through me. I had been wanting to say that to Cassie for half my life. It felt good to set her straight, even if she did look like a kid who'd had her Halloween candy stolen.

"That went well," I said. But Lana was smirking.

"What?"

"I thought your plan was to tell people what they wanted to hear?"

She had a point. "Okay, but this was different. I've been wanting to tell Cassie that all year."

"Right, but if you were truly in this only to make money, you would've told her William is secretly in love with her. Right?"

I snorted. "Not even I could sell that load of dump."

"I don't think that's it," said Lana. "You're not a scammer, Geo. You don't like lying to people. And I don't think you *are* lying to people."

I planted my face in my hands. "Oh, come on, not that Feather junk again. You can't seriously be—"

"Shhh!" said Lana, pointing.

Feather was coming. Worse than coming. "Is she *skipping*?" I asked, barely containing my disgust.

"She is definitely skipping," confirmed Lana.

Her multicolor skirt puffed and swung around her legs as she bobbed like a deranged Mary Poppins underneath Lana's ridiculous purple umbrella.

"I'm doing it!" she sang as she got within shouting range. Her hair was wisping out of two short, sloppy braids. Her smile was megawatt. "See? I'm spending the day outside!"

"That's great!" said Lana. "Isn't it, Geo?"

I opened my mouth, then closed it again.

"I'm not usually an outside-in-the-summer person," continued Feather as she reached our table, then circled it as she twirled. "But I figured I'd better do what Geo said."

Her enthusiasm was leaking everywhere, making my stomach tight. I'd forgotten all about telling her that. And maybe Lana was right that I didn't like making stuff up, because right now I wanted to take it all back. "Feather, I might have given you the wrong advice."

She stopped in front of me, her smile losing a few watts. "What do you mean?"

"You shouldn't just do something because some random psychic says to do it. You should do it because *you* want to do it. Or because it makes sense."

"But because of you I *do* want to do it."

"Look," I heard myself say. "What if Jade wasn't lying? What if I'm making it all up?" I had been seized by a sudden urge to tell this flaky girl the truth, the whole truth, and nothing but the truth.

Lana shot me a *what-the-heck-are-you-doing?* look. And maybe if we hadn't been interrupted, I really would've confessed everything. But before I could, Zafirah shouted from across the park. "Geo! You were right! I found him! He was there!" She was hurrying toward us with a posse of girls and something long, thick, and white draped over her arms. When she got closer she raised it up triumphantly and I realized what it was: an enormous albino python, its head waving high in the air, looking at me. A wave of chills went up my spine.

"Harold," I croaked, my mouth suddenly dry.

"He was exactly where you said he'd be!" Zafirah was still shouting, even though she and Harold were now right in front of me. "Curled up behind the litter, just like you said!"

"See?" said Feather. "You were right."

Clearly. The problem was, I was even more right than Feather knew. I had *seen* that snake. How could that be? It was impossible!

I couldn't think about that now. I had to pull myself together and perform. Some of Zafirah's entourage were not just watching, they were filming. How I responded could make the difference between big success and HUGE success. So I went into performer mode, looking from camera to camera.

"The rocks never lie. Only ten dollars per reading. Come to the park and line up by the yellow dinosaur!"

"She's not lying," said Zafirah, the cameras swinging to catch her giant grin. She held Harold toward the cameras. "She saved Harold's life! Come see for yourself!"

Zafirah ran off with Harold. Her friends who stayed pushed their way into line. Lana was giving me a new look now, one I was about to start seeing a lot of, that said, *so how do you explain that?*

Meanwhile, Feather simply beamed. "I told you you're amazing!"

"Thanks, Feather." I hoped no one could see how shaky I was feeling underneath my wildly beating heart.

She leaned in close and whispered, "Doubting yourself is super normal. Sometimes even the best psychics in the world wonder if they're making it up." Then, before I could stop her, she tossed her umbrella to the ground, threw her arms around me, and squeezed. "That's why we need true friends. They remind us who we really are."

CHAPTER 18

Feather let me go and Lana snickered behind her hand as she watched me recover from the sudden onslaught of Feathery affection. I'm not a hugger, to put it mildly. But I'm a professional, so I managed to shake it off and get back to the task at hand.

Thanks to Zafirah Jackson, I barely had time the rest of the day to drink or pee, and the next few days were the same. It seemed like as soon as one customer left, another would come. This was good, and not just for business. Because it meant I didn't have time to think. If I had had time to think, I would have asked myself what the heck was happening. If I had attempted to answer, I would have gotten so freaked out I would have quit.

Instead, I turned the asking-questions part of my brain off completely and focused only on the money we were making. Every night I'd lie on my bed tallying up the amount we'd made. From forty-two dollars that first day we'd jumped to hundreds a day. At the rate we were going, Rock Reading was going to be an even bigger moneymaker than I'd dreamed.

The work was exhausting, but not especially hard. Kids mostly asked about the usual: crushes, friends, grades, sports, and winning. "Will I pass science this year?" "Are we going to reach the finals?" "Am I ever going to be famous on YouTube?" Several kids, whispering, wanted to know if I could make them popular. Most of those kids were just in need of good, solid advice and maybe a few wake-up calls. I barely paid attention to the rocks in those cases. I simply told them what they needed to hear.

Others were different. When they asked something unexpected, something where the answer wasn't easy or obvious, was when the rocks helped the most. And when the weird stuff tended to happen.

Like a ten-year-old named Alejandro who'd spent half his life begging his mother for a kitten. His mom kept saying "maybe later" and "now's not a good time," and he wanted to know if it would happen and when. He pulled the orange citrine and a chunk of black-and-white onyx. I looked at the rocks until the colors swam together, orange, black, and white, and voilà! I was seeing a fuzzy calico kitten. I imagined him holding the kitten, kissing its soft little head, and snuggling it into his chest. Along with the image came a feeling of coziness, warmth, and certainty.

"It'll happen," I said. "Soon." I described the kitten, right down to its blue eyes, pink nose, and fuzzy white chest. That wasn't the weird part, of course. The weird part was when an old lady the very next day asked us if she could hang a flyer on our easel. A flyer for free kittens. Third kitten from the left? You guessed it: a fluffy calico with blue eyes, pink nose, and fuzzy white chest. Feather, in a fit of squeals, raced with Lana to find Alejandro. And for some reason no one can explain, Alejandro's mother finally said yes.

Boom. Kitten for Alejandro.

Every time something like that happened, Feather would cheer like I had made a goal, and Lana would give me The Look. As for me, I worked like a machine, going on autopilot from one to the next, barely stopping to breathe. At times it felt like I wasn't even there, like my thinking, rational self had been sucked into another dimension, letting some other, deeper part of me take over instead. They'd pick rocks, and if it wasn't the kind of question I could answer with common sense advice, Lana would whisper a few facts in my ear, and images would start flashing. Or, sometimes not even images, but ideas. Stuff that I suddenly *knew*. Most of the time what came out of my mouth surprised even me.

Like my last reading on that last day, the day before everything changed.

It was midafternoon and, fittingly, a storm was brewing. I was doing a reading for this cute pudgy kid with giant glasses, maybe around ten years old. He was someone's cousin visiting from Vermont, so I'd never even seen him before. Turns out his favorite grandpa had died a few months back. I knew he was missing him bad because his eyes welled up as he told me this.

"That stinks," I said, which it did. "I'm really sorry. But I'm not sure what you're asking."

"Just, um," he mumbled, picking at the worn edge of his T-shirt. "Like, is he still out there? Can he see me?"

What the heck, kid, I wanted to say. You're asking me about dead people?

"Psychics aren't always mediums," piped up Feather, saving me. She turned to me with a question on her face. "Of course some are gifted at both. Do you have mediumship abilities, too, Geo?"

I rubbed my forehead, distracted by a flashback to the night I'd asked my dad for help figuring out how to make money. The whole reason I was sitting out here being a Rock Reader was because of my dad and the video of him. Except surely that hadn't *really* been him helping me. It was just a desperate prayer followed by a weird coincidence. Wasn't it? These were exactly the kind of thoughts I was trying to avoid.

I was still sitting there like a ding-head, rubbing my hair into a frizz, not answering Feather.

Lana saved me. "Go ahead and pick a rock," she urged the boy gently. "Anything can happen in a Rock Reading."

I smiled at her gratefully. That was exactly the answer I would have given had my brain not shorted out. Eventually, the kid picked up the smoky quartz and a cube of golden pyrite. Before he'd even handed them to me, I got a flash of an old guy with a bristly beard, wearing a rumpled green fisherman's cap covered in those funny little fake-fly lures they put on the end of a fishing pole. The flies were glinting in beams of golden sunlight, and he was chewing a pipe. Pretty stereotypical grandad, but I went with it.

"Did your grandpa fish?" I asked, palming the rocks in my hand.

"Yeah," said the kid, lighting up. "Fly-fishing. He loved it."

The man in the image pointed to his pipe. "And did he smoke a pipe?" I asked.

"Yes!" he said, leaning forward.

Now Grandpa was pointing to his nose. *Smell that?* he seemed to be saying.

"He's pointing to his nose. Did you like how it smelled?" I asked.

Wide eyed, the kid nodded, and words rushed out. "It was my favorite. My mom hated when he smoked around me, but he'd go sit on this old blue milk crate in his driveway and I'd sneak out and sit with him. I still smell it sometimes, even when no one's around. Like on my way here. Just over there by the street. It just kind of comes out of nowhere. When I smell it, that's him, isn't it? I knew it. It's really him!"

The grandpa in my head gave a big thumbs-up.

For some reason, the sight of the old guy beaming at me like we were sharing a joke was the thing that finally put me over the edge. That and the fact that the guy in my mind had been sitting in a driveway on an old blue milk crate.

My head screamed, "Stop!" and immediately the old guy went poof and disappeared. I opened my eyes, dropped the rocks on the table like they were hot, and grasped the sides of it, trying to keep myself steady.

"Um, yeah, that was him all right," I said. I was doing my best to keep my professional cool going, but my voice was strained. Had a dead guy been communicating with me? For real? *"Not possible!"* screamed the sane, rational part of me that was trying to claw its way back into control.

The boy stared. "Is that it?"

"Is that it?" I snapped. "I just *saw* your grandpa. *In my freaking mind.* He sends you stinking smoke signals. What more do you want from me?"

He shrunk back. "I just meant if you're done?"

I realized I was standing. Slowly, I sat back down. "Sorry. Yeah, I'm done. You can go now."

There were at least a dozen kids waiting in line. As much as we needed that money, I just couldn't do it. "Sorry, that's it for today. We're closed. Come back tomorrow."

Some of the kids in line grumbled. Others looked kind of scared.

"You're as pale as my marble," said Lana.

"If that was your first time being a medium, you'll need time to clear your aura and recharge," said Feather. "And make sure the spirit hasn't attached to you, of course. They do that sometimes, even when they're nice. I recommend a good space clearing, followed by a sea salt bath, then finish up with some grounding exercises." She patted me on the back, then called out to the kids who were slowly dispersing. "Tell all your friends! Geo isn't just a psychic, she's a medium, too!"

I closed my eyes and tried to make the world stop spinning. If that had been real, and I had communicated with a dead guy, what did it mean? Did it mean I really could actually talk to my dad? And what was that part about it attaching to me?

No. No. No!

Stop it, I said to myself. I was being absurd. Lots of grandpas fished and smoked pipes. It was a coincidence, just like everything else. And in any case, I had to keep myself together. I had weeks of Rock Reading still to come.

"They sure fell for that," I whispered to Lana with a shaky smile.

Before she could even roll her eyes, someone shrieked from across the park.

CHAPTER 19

Jade.

She was heading my way in a storm cloud of drama, followers swirling in her wake like leaves in a breeze. I braced for attack as she raged toward me, ten feet away, then five, then two . . .

"You witch!" she spat, a foot from my nose. Except she didn't really say *witch*. Her word started with a different letter.

All I did was say, "Yes?" Which actually isn't all that bad of a comeback if you think about it. If someone calls you a witch with a *B* you might as well own it.

She leaned in close and hissed, "You *knew*."

That left me genuinely at a loss. "What are you talking about?"

"Cal-i-for-ni-a," she seethed, like each syllable was its own word.

Chills went up my back. Her reading felt like it was weeks ago, but it had only been a few days. It was easy to remember the image I'd had of booting her up into the air, and her landing with a big, satisfying poof in a forest in California. It had been a gratifying vision.

"You *knew*," she said again, and jammed a paper into my chest. A brochure for a boarding school, I saw, my eyes scanning down. A boarding school . . . in the mountains of California.

What? I opened my mouth then shut it again. *This was not possible.* I stood there dumbly as phones recorded my every move. Feather stepped up to fill the gap. "I don't get it," she said, her voice nervous but steady. "First you said she was a fake, now you think she's *too* good? Why are you so mad, anyway? You should never blame a psychic for a correct prediction. She only saw what would happen. It's not like she made it happen."

Jade hissed a breath out through her nostrils like an angry bull getting ready to charge. Feather shrunk back. For a moment I thought Jade might actually attack us physically when, suddenly, her face changed. I could practically see a light bulb flash over her head as her mouth turned up into an evil Grinch-style grin. She whirled around to face the phones.

"But that's exactly what she did. Don't you see? How else does she get so many of her predictions right? I thought she was a scammer at first, but now I realize it's much worse than that. Even the best psychic in the world is wrong sometimes. And since when was she ever a psychic, anyway? No one becomes one overnight. What she's doing is unnatural."

There were twitters as the kids around us tried to figure out where, exactly, she was going with this. It was easy to see why she was so successful as an influencer. The atmosphere itself seemed to shift as she spoke. "Geo didn't *predict* I was going to California. She's *sending* me there."

I forced out a laugh. "Don't be ridiculous." The idea that I was somehow responsible for Jade going to California was absurd. How could I possibly do something like that? But my attempt to sound unfazed wasn't working. My laugh came out dry as sticks, and Jade was staring at me like she was the one who could read minds. Worse, she could sense my weakness, and she was going to use it.

She whirled around, back in full command. "Am I being ridiculous? *Am I?* Because this isn't ridiculous to me. It's my *life.*" She snatched the brochure back from me and held it in the air. "She's no ordinary psychic, people." She pointed at me like we were in some ridiculous Puritan-era movie. "She's a witch!"

This time, the word started with a *W*, not a *B*, and somehow that was worse. The kids on the playground had gone quiet. I coughed out another laugh, but no one laughed with me. I turned, desperately, to Lana. But she wasn't laughing either. Instead, her dark eyes searched mine.

It was Feather who finally broke the silence. "Um . . ." She cleared her throat. "What's wrong with being a witch?"

"There! They admitted it!" said Jade, triumphant.

Everyone started talking at once. It was official: I had lost control completely. If I was going to grab any of it back, I had to do something, fast. I shook myself into fighting mode and stood up to my full, very short height. "Have you people lost your minds? Are you seriously accusing me of witchcraft? Snap out of it. There's no such thing as witches!"

"Of course there are," whispered Feather. "I've met several. They were very nice."

"Not now!" I hissed.

"Think about it," said Jade. "Witches talk to snakes, right?" Several of the kids nodded. Looking around, I realized the youngest Jackson sister had shown up with what might have been an entire scout club's worth of friends. If they had been older maybe they would have laughed and broke the tension, but they were young enough to believe anything. Jade caught sight of her, too. "She knew *exactly* where your sister's snake was, right? And didn't she get that kid a cat, too, practically out of thin air?"

Everyone was eating it up, and the cameras were catching all of it.

"What the dunk is wrong with all of you!" I said hotly.

Jade's eyes narrowed. "She's a witch."

"Come on! First she says I'm fake, now she thinks I cast spells? She's clearly just trying to tank us. If anyone's a witch, it's Jade!" I sputtered. I sounded desperate, even to myself.

"Witch!" she repeated, her eyes boring into mine.

Feather looked bewildered. "Um, I still don't get it. Witches aren't bad."

"The ones who practice dark magic are. This Rock Reading business is a lie!" Jade, feeling the win and high on the drama, marched to our easel and grasped the edge of the first page, the one that said Rock Readers on it. "She made a deal with the devil, and now she's cursing all of you!"

If drama was what she wanted, she got more than she ever dreamed of when she tore off our sign and underneath was the drawing Manuel had made. The drawing of a witch. A drawing that, now that I was seeing it again, was absolutely, clearly, 100 percent me.

I'm not kidding, someone actually screamed.

"Aha!" Jade pointed like she was the main character of a movie in her moment of triumph.

I had to end this, now. I climbed up on my chair. It wobbled for a second, but Lana quickly grabbed the back and held me steady.

"That's it!" I shouted. "We're closed! Get out of here, all of you!" No one moved. They just kept watching me, and a few phones stayed pointed on me, too.

I gave them my best glare and made my voice extra menacing. "I. Said. Go."

Still, nothing. No one was going anywhere until Jade did, that much was clear. And that's when I realized her mistake. By going all in on accusing me of being a curse-wielding witch, she'd backed herself into a corner. She told everyone I was a dark-magic-using witch, so that's exactly what she'd get. Still standing on my chair, I reached out my hand and said, "Lana, hand me the lizardite."

Lana didn't hesitate. She grabbed the slimy green rock from the table and pressed it silently into my palm. I held it high over my head so everyone could see, then pointed it straight between Jade's eyes. "Fine. You think I cursed you?" I gave her a sickly sweet smile. "Then what makes you think I won't do it again? I can do a lot worse than some school in a forest. Have you ever heard of Death Valley? I'll bet you can guess what state it's in."

Jade's eyes widened, just for a millisecond, before she recovered. "Are you threatening me, witch?"

"Yes, I am. And if you really believe what you say, that should scare the pee out of you." I lifted the lizardite back above my head. "I'm giving you ten seconds. If I were you, I'd run. Ten, nine, eight . . ."

Challenging Jade like that was a huge risk. Thank gourd it worked. She made an *I'll-get-you-for-this* face, then turned and stalked off, her followers scampering to keep up.

I turned to everyone else. "What are you waiting for? I said we're closed!" They scattered. Even Feather was slinking away until I hopped off the chair and grabbed her shoulder. "Not you. You can stay."

She looked close to crying. "I'm so sorry. Me and my dumb mouth. That was all my fault. I should have told them you weren't a witch."

I sighed. "It wasn't your fault in the least. Trust me, that was all Jade."

For a moment I was afraid she was going to hug me again. If Feather truly thought I was a witch, it sure didn't seem to bother her. "That whole thing was insane," she gushed. "It was like watching a movie. Jade is scary, but you were even scarier. It was downright theatrical! Look, I think you made actual storm clouds come!"

Feather was right, dark clouds had gathered over the trees past my house. But Lana didn't even turn her head. "Give me the rock," she said, holding out her hand.

I handed it over.

"Now," she said, pointing to my chair, "sit. And talk."

CHAPTER 20

I sat down with a grunt. That's about all anyone can do when confronted with a stubborn Lana. A stubborn Lana didn't happen often, but when it did, you obeyed her.

Lana placed the lizardite back in its place. "You too, Feather. Sit."

Feather sat. Lana stood at her full height, towering over us. "We're going to talk about this."

"Look, I know Jade is going to get me back for that, and that's bad. But she left me no choice!"

"I don't mean Jade. I'm talking about the predictions, Geo. Why could you see that kid's grandfather? And how are all your predictions coming true?"

"I have no idea," I admitted, glancing nervously at Feather.

Feather wrinkled her forehead, then cleared her throat. "I don't understand. Of course they're coming true. You're super talented. Or, wait, are you worried you really are a witch?"

I shifted uncomfortably.

"Because you can't be a witch without choosing to be one," she said earnestly. "And the way you held that rock up to curse them? That's not how a real witch would do it at all."

"Thanks, Feather," I said weakly.

"Real witches hardly ever curse anyone. They believe that everything they send out comes back at them times three. It's a wicca thing. They call it the Rule of Three. So if they curse someone else, they get cursed three times worse."

I groaned. Just what I needed, witchcraft philosophy from a Feather brain.

Lana was looking at me pointedly. "We need to tell her."

Feather's eyebrows lifted. "Tell me what?"

I stared at my hands, then looked out at the sky. The dark clouds over the trees had gotten closer. "There's definitely a storm coming. We've got to pack up."

"She knows things about this," said Lana, ignoring me. "Feather can tell us what's going on."

"Please no. I can't deal with any more voodoo today."

"Voodoo?" Feather repeated. "There was no voodoo today, either. That's—" She stopped to wrinkle her forehead. "I hope you're not making fun of voodoo, because it's a real religion practiced by—"

"Oh for junk's sake, stop!" I had finally hit my limit, just as the first sound of thunder rolled in the distance. "Don't you see? It's *all* voodoo. All of it."

Feather's giant anime eyes were filling with confusion. "Why are you being super offensive about voodoo all of a sudden?"

"Forget about the stinking voodoo already! We've been lying to you, Feather. Wake up and smell the feldspar. Jade was right. Not about the witch thing, but what she said at first, about me being a con artist. I'm making the whole thing up. I'm a fraud."

There were a lot of reactions I was expecting just then. Feather could have stomped off. Or screamed. Cursed me out. Or worse, cried. I definitely wasn't expecting her to laugh. "Silly Geo. You're literally the best psychic I've ever met. If you're not the real deal, then no one is."

"Stop it!" I said. "You're not listening. I made the whole thing up so I could make money. I'm a scammer, Feather. And I hate to tell you this, but so are all the other psychics, too."

There, I thought. *Now she'll get it*. But Feather only sat back and folded her arms. "Oh, please. You're just scared."

"Ugh! Tell her, Lana."

Lana nodded, then looked Feather in the eyes and said, gently, "Geo's right that it did start out that way. We meant it to be a scam, just to make some money." She glanced at me. "But I don't think it's a scam anymore. I think it's real."

Feather looked from me to Lana and back again.

"I'm sorry we lied to you." I tried to sound apologetic, but there were so many emotions rolling around in me it came out sounding almost angry instead.

Feather screwed up her face, squeezing her eyes shut. "Give me a minute," she said, holding up her finger. We sat in silence, as another clap of thunder rolled in the distance. Finally, her eyes popped open. "Okay. I forgive you!"

"What?"

"I forgive you."

"I lied to you day after day, and you forgive me? Just like that?"

She shrugged. "The important thing is that you know you're the real deal now. It's my job to help you see it. Then you can stop lying to yourself."

I tried to laugh, but it came out sounding dry and harsh like a strangled chipmunk.

I looked to Lana for help but she wasn't laughing at all. She focused her dark eyes on me. "Geo, I agree with her."

Great. My best, oldest, and most rational friend had fully crossed to the Feather side of life. "This cannot be happening. Listen to yourself. I'm a *scammer*. You *know* that." I looked around desperately, as if I could find proof. "That ridiculous umbrella!" I sputtered, pointing to it. "She's been carrying that thing all week for absolutely no reason." I turned back to Feather. "Aren't you embarrassed?"

Feather only shrugged. "Why should I be? You were right about it. It helped me stay outside, and staying outside helped me make friends." She gave me and Lana one of her giant doe-eyed smiles. "I love this umbrella!"

I put my head on the table.

Lana gave me a moment, then spoke gently. "I can tell when you're scamming someone, Geo. When you're giving your readings? It's completely different."

Feather nodded. "I feel it too. The energy shifts." I grunted with frustration but she persisted. "All energy workers have a story about how they first discovered their gifts. This is your story!"

I dropped my forehead several more times onto the table. "I am not an energy worker! This is not my story!"

Lana crossed her arms. "Fine. Then you explain it."

I stared down at my hands curled up on my lap, full of feelings I couldn't name. All at once I had an urgent need to get away from them. I had to speak with someone rational. Someone reliable. Someone who could tell the difference between reality and ridiculousness, who would give me a straight answer, not just a bunch more questions. I needed Alan. Lightning flickered as I pulled out my phone and texted, **"I need to talk. 911."**

Lana looked at me sideways. "What are you doing?"

"I need to talk to someone who hasn't lost all their brains." I had meant it to sound light, like a joke, but it came out sharp as flint. Lana folded her arms and stared at me, her eyes dark and stubborn. "Come on," I said. "It really is starting to storm. We all need to get out of here."

My phone dinged. **"RU hurt? Where RU?"**

"Not hurt need to talk can u meet at Beans?" Beans was my favorite of our local coffee shops, and Alan had been taking me there forever.

"Be there in ten" came the reply. I shoved my phone back in my pocket and got up to go.

Lana's expression was as fierce as the storm cloud rolling in. "Seriously? You're walking away?"

My temper took over. "Maybe I just need to talk to someone who hasn't been completely brainwashed by woo," I snapped, glaring at Feather.

Instead of looking insulted, Feather's face twisted with concern. Unlike me and Lana, her voice came out soft. "It's okay to be scared. That's normal. You're going to be all right."

I exhaled so hard I practically hissed. "Quit it with the touchy-feely, would you? Give it a rest for half a second. You don't know anything about me. You're *not* my friend." As soon as I'd said it, I hated myself for it. But I couldn't take it back.

Lana took it back for me. "Don't listen to her," she said, glaring at me hard. "Geo's not as mean as she sounds. She just needs a time-out."

"Yeah, that's exactly what I need," I said. As I stormed away, the first drops of rain began to fall.

CHAPTER 21

By the time I had stomped my way to the coffee shop, I was a soaking wet mess, but the walk had done me some good. My breathing had returned to normal and my temper was coming back to within normal range, too. Already I was regretting what I'd said and how I'd said it, but I was not regretting my decision to talk to Alan. He was smart and rational, and I desperately needed both.

I wiped a wet mix of sweat and rain off my forehead with the sleeve of my T-shirt, feeling about as elegant as a drowned Yorkie. When I saw Alan, it was like he was living in an entirely different season, with pressed khaki pants, a button-down shirt neatly tucked in, and brown leather shoes. Sure, his hair was a little extra tufty from the humidity, and his glasses were all fogged up, but there wasn't a gleam of sweat on him.

"Do you even have sweat glands?" I greeted him.

Relief flooded into his face when he saw me, and his entire body relaxed. My texts must have scared him pretty bad. Thankfully he didn't seem mad about it. Instead, he chuckled as he opened the door. "You might see the evidence if we don't go straight in."

The cold air hit me like an invisible wall. "Oh thank gourd," I said, flapping my shirt to air it out. Inside, boring people ordered normal drinks, sat at ordinary plastic tables and talked about boring things. Not a whiff of incense and not a crystal in sight. To everyone in this place, I was just a regular sweaty kid. It helped me feel more like me again.

I ordered my favorite summer drink, an iced hot chocolate, which no matter what anyone says is *not at all* the same thing as chocolate milk, and slid gratefully into a cool booth. Alan got a plain coffee with cream. "So . . . what's going on?"

Now that he was there in front of me, I didn't have a clue where to start. "Ugh, I don't even know . . ." I shook my head. "It's dumb. I'm sorry I bothered you."

"Never ever be sorry about reaching out to me. That's what I'm here for."

"Thanks, Alan."

"Let me guess. Jade?"

"Well . . . partly. She came to the park again this morning and called me a witch with a *B*. Then she called me an actual witch."

He winced. "I am so sorry. That is absolutely not okay."

I gathered my courage, took a breath, and plunged ahead. "But it's not just about Jade. It's this whole Rock Reading thing. It's gotten out of control."

Alan nodded. "I see. How so?"

I took a moment to stir the whipped cream into my drink. "Well, we're making tons of money, so that part is good. But..." I hesitated again. No part of me wanted to say the next words, but I forced them out anyway. This was the entire reason I'd called him here, after all. "It's my predictions. They're coming true."

He leaned back, laughing appreciatively. "Awesome."

"No, you don't get it..." I stopped stirring my drink as rain spattered hard against the window. "I'm not kidding. They're *all* coming true. That's why she called me a witch. Everyone thinks I'm a witch, for real."

He waved this off. "Good! Let them think you're a witch. Since when do you care what other people think?"

"Right, it's just . . ." My shoulders slumped. This was harder than I thought it would be. "It's freaking me out. Even Lana thinks something weird is happening, and she's one of the smartest people I know."

"Ahhhhhhh," he said, drawing it way out. "I see."

"But she's not wrong, Alan. Like, weird stuff really IS happening. Not just a few things came true. It's nearly everything. And then I talked to this kid's dead grandpa, and—"

His eyes widened and he held up his hand. "Okay, um, stop right there." He waited till I got quiet, then continued. "Let me guess. You made some predictions, just for fun. Then a couple weird coincidences happened, which were easy to write off. But then there was another, and then another and another. Right?"

I sat up straighter. "Exactly."

"Coincidences that seemed impossible. Coincidences that you couldn't explain."

"Yes!"

"There's actually a name for that. You know what it is?"

I leaned forward. "What?"

"Coincidence."

I let my head drop onto my arms. "Real helpful, Alan. Thanks."

"No," he said, growing even more earnest. "I'm serious. People are always getting spooked by coincidence. What they don't realize is that coincidences, even truly bizarre ones, are statistically inevitable. Literally impossible to avoid."

I picked up my head. "But you don't get it. This wasn't just one. It was—"

"An impossible, ridiculous string of them?"

I nodded.

"Yes," he continued, leaning forward. "Even repeated, truly absurd coincidences are perfectly normal. Don't let that make you go soft in the brain." He tapped the side of his head. "Stay rational. Be like your dad and me. You'll understand better when you get to college and study statistics. Honestly, if more people studied statistics, the reduction in overall world stupidity would be considerable."

I nodded again, my heart heavy. Because of course he was right. And hearing him mention my dad had brought a sudden, sharp sting of shame. What would he think of me now? I had actually fallen for my own scam. What a joke. Anyone who mixed up a bunch of coincidences with some kind of woo-woo magic was as dumb as the rocks they were reading.

"Hey," said Alan. "Don't be hard on yourself. You're not the first smart person to be lured by the fantastical."

"Thanks," I said, stirring my drink as I stared out the window. I felt like I was crashing back down to earth, which, of course, was exactly why I had called Alan. I'd needed someone to plant me back on solid ground, back to where I knew what was real and what was not. And talking to Alan had done that. Heck, even the rain was coming down far gentler now, like it, too, had been tamed by logic.

So why didn't I feel any better? Instead, I was getting cold and shivery, on the inside as well as the out.

"You need dry clothes," said Alan. "Let's get you home." He took one last swig of coffee, then we dropped off our cups in the dirty dish bin and walked out into the steamy aftermath of the storm.

"You don't have to walk with me," I said.

"Of course I don't have to. I'd be honored to." He gave me a fake gallant bow. After a couple of blocks, he looked down and said, "If I know you, you'll take the witch angle and run with it." He worked up his best imitation of an evil grin. "Hot tip: The real money's in curse removal. Convince someone they've got a curse, then charge them a bundle to remove it. People will sell their own teeth to remove a curse."

"Alan, that's terrible!" I said, half laughing.

"Well it is for them because then they're both stupid *and* toothless."

That time I laughed for real.

"I'm just messing with you," he continued. "I mean, that kind of scam does work, and if anyone could pull it off you could. But it's deeply unethical. Which, speaking of ethics . . . have you given that your full consideration yet?"

"Sure. I mean, sort of. Kinda. I guess?"

"That was convincing," he said, raising his eyebrows.

We'd reached my house and he walked me all the way to the rickety front porch, the old wood planks moaning as I headed up. I turned at the top and said, "Thanks for putting my head back on." Then I saw him there blinking at me through his little fogged-up glasses and suddenly ran back down the steps to give him a quick side squeeze. "Thanks for everything," I said, pressing my cheek briefly against his arm. It was a quick hug, but I hoped he knew that I meant it 100 percent, and not just for everything today, but for an entire lifetime of everything.

Judging by the smile he gave me before he turned to walk away, he did.

CHAPTER 22

I pulled the rickety screen door shut behind me, ready to collapse on my bed for another good, long think. The tap-tap-tapping of my mom's nails on her computer keyboard in the laundry room signaled to me that she was working, so I headed straight up the steps to my room without interrupting her. I checked my phone to see if Lana had texted, and tried not to worry too much when I saw she hadn't.

I knew I should probably be the one to text first. But what should I say? Thanks to Alan I was on firm ground again, anchored safely to reason and reality. I was embarrassed for giving Feather's New Age magic woo stuff even an ounce of thought. But how would I say that without getting into an argument all over again?

Besides, I had other things to think about. Like Jade. I was sure she didn't believe in witchcraft or woo either, but that didn't seem to matter. The whole California thing put her in full combat mode, and that was bad, because her weapons were a lot sharper than mine.

"Thank gourd for you, Fridgie," I said, standing in front of my air conditioner and holding my T-shirt out to catch his chilly air. But before my sweat could dry, I heard a knock at my door and my mom ask, "Hey, Scuzz Booty. Can I come in?"

"Yes?" I called, curious.

The door opened and I caught my breath. "Oh my gourd, what did you do to your hair?"

"You like?" she asked, coming all the way in the room. She pretended to give it a pat. "I look like a normal mom now, don't I?"

My mom's hair color changed by the week, if not by the day, but I couldn't remember a time that it had ever been a flat, boring shade of brown. Then I realized she'd taken all her piercings out, too. "You look . . . suburban?"

"Ouch," she said.

"Sorry, but . . ." Well, she did. She looked like . . . like someone who worked a regular job. "Oh no," I said, dread pooling in my gut. "You have an interview."

"It's almost like you're psychic." She winked.

I ignored the joke. She let her smile drop away, then cleared her throat and sat gently on my bed. "Geo, listen. It's a good job. With benefits and everything. We'd have security. *Real* security."

"Where is it?" I asked, the dread getting even heavier.

She hesitated. "Minneapolis."

"Minne-WHAT?!?!"

"The interview is in two days," she continued, speaking quickly. "I was just booking a flight when you came in . . . for tomorrow."

"TOMORROW?!"

"Listen—"

"No, you listen!" I said. "Absolutely not." I paced back and forth in front of my old brown bed. "This is NOT okay."

"I realize this is hard, but—"

"Stop!" I said, breathing fast. "You don't have to do this." I stopped pacing, an idea hitting me over the head like a sledgehammer. Why hadn't I thought of this before? "Ask Alan for help! He has tons of money, he—"

"No," she said. "I can't, Bug Breath."

"Of course you can!"

"No, I can't. Because . . . I already did."

"Wait—what? He didn't say no, did he? Alan would never say no."

"Geo, please. Sit down." She sat on my bed and patted next to her.

I lowered myself down stiff as a board. She closed her eyes for a moment, then began. "After the economy tanked, when jobs started drying up, I took out a mortgage on the house. Do you know what a mortgage is?"

"A loan," I said, my stomach clenching. "With your house as collateral."

She nodded. "I took out a mortgage with the bank, planning to pay it off as soon as work picked up again, but it never picked up." She swallowed. "I fell behind on some payments and a few months ago I got a foreclosure notice. Basically, we were going to be kicked out of our house."

"Kicked out?" My throat felt like it was closing. "Where would we go?"

"Exactly. That's when I asked Alan for help. For money. And he gave it."

"So what's the problem?" I asked, feeling my jaw tense.

She took a deep breath and let it out. "He's a dear friend, Geo. Very dear. But it was wrong of me to ask. It's way too much. He's saving up to have his own family one day. He shouldn't be funding ours."

"But we *are* his family. I'm basically his daughter, he's said so himself like a million times."

"Which is exactly why we can't take advantage of him," she said. "He'd never refuse us, but it would be wrong."

"Fine, so we'll pay him back! I'm making tons of money. We can draw up a contract and everything, pay in installments."

Her shoulders sank. "Geo—"

"No! Mom, listen. I'm good at this. For real. You have to trust me. I can do this. Please!"

Underneath her mud-brown hair, her eyes were giant puddles of sadness. "I'm doing the interview, kiddo. I'm sorry."

She foisted a big soppy hug on me, which I stiffened against, then stood up to leave. But I wasn't done. "I'm going to prove it to you. I'm going to make so much money you won't need to say yes to that job. You won't need to say yes to any job you don't want to do."

She turned at the door. "I love you, sweetie."

When my mom calls me sweetie, that's when I know it's bad. "We're *not* going to Minneapolis," I growled as she closed the door.

I picked up my phone to text Lana, then put it back down and curled into a little ball on my bed. There was only one thing that could fix this, and that was money. We'd made $422 so far, which wasn't bad. Actually, it was pretty amazing. But we still needed to make a lot more, and faster.

Maybe Alan was right. Maybe I could make this whole witch thing work to my advantage.

CHAPTER 23

The thing about skipping dinner is that you wake up the next morning feeling like someone scraped out your guts with a serving spoon. When I woke up, it was pitch-dark and I was tangled in the sheets on my bed, still wearing the same clothes as the day before. Groggy and confused, I fumbled for my phone and checked the time. Five a.m.? What on earth? For some reason my mom let me sleep all the way through dinner. I was way too hungry to wait another minute, so I stumbled downstairs and half blindly shoved a frozen bagel into the toaster oven.

I was resting my forehead against the nice, cool countertop when suddenly the garage door rumbled and headlights flooded the kitchen with light. It could only be Alan, but what the heck was he doing here this early? I heard the car door slam and waited for him to come into the kitchen, but when the side door opened it wasn't Alan who walked in.

It was Jade.

"Good morning, cupcake!" she said, showing all her teeth.

You know when people say "the world tilted"? I always assumed it was just an expression, but the shock of Jade Sinclair standing there in my kitchen made me so dizzy I had to grab the counter to stay upright.

Before I could even process it, Alan came through the door behind her, a brown duffel bag over his shoulder and a huge *sorry* on his face.

"Rae?" he called upstairs. "You ready?" Above me, I heard a muffled cry, then several thumps.

My ears rang as all the blood left my head, but I managed to somehow stay upright and ask, "What is going on?"

He dropped the bag on the floor. Behind his glasses, his eyes widened in panic. "Didn't your mom tell you?"

Jade, leaning casually against the refrigerator, barked out a laugh. "She doesn't know!"

Heat rose in my face, which had the fortunate side effect of sending blood back into my brain. But no amount of fresh oxygen could help me make sense of my current situation. "Tell me what? Alan, what is *she* doing here?"

He sighed. "Let me bring the rest of our things inside and I'll explain."

The kitchen filled with the smell of burnt bagel as behind me, the toaster dinged. I ignored it, keeping my eye on Jade, who was now slithering around the room, her eyes crawling over everything. "Who picked that color for your walls?" she asked, looking as if she'd spotted a cockroach.

Her voice was innocent but I knew exactly what she was up to. "That trick doesn't work on me."

"Excuse me?" she asked.

"It's something manipulators do. They make little comments and observations about you or your stuff to make you see it differently, as a way of getting in your head. Like, literally no one cares what color my kitchen walls are. It doesn't matter at all. You're just trying to give me something to feel insecure about, to put me off balance. It won't work."

"God you're weird," she said. She kept looking around, her lips curling in disgust. "Seriously, though, is that their real color, or are they just covered in mold?" She gave a little shudder. "Is *anything* in here actually clean?"

"Jade!" Alan snapped as he shuffled back into the room holding an army-green duffel bag. He sounded shocked and disappointed at once. He dropped his bag to the kitchen floor. "I'm so sorry, Geo. This is not how this was supposed to go."

Before I could answer we heard footsteps rushing toward us, and my mom flew into the kitchen in a wrinkled gray pantsuit, dragging a little rolling suitcase behind her. "Oh my god oh my god oh my god I'm late I'm late I'm late," she chanted as she ran to the cupboard and popped a handful of trail mix into her mouth. "I overslept by a mile." She turned to Alan. "You ready?"

"Wait," I said. "You're leaving for your interview NOW?"

Behind me, Jade clapped with glee. "She's figuring it out!"

"I'm so sorry, Slug Breath," said my mom, combing her hair with her fingers as she peered at her reflection in the microwave window.

I cut her off, grabbing her arm. "Mom. *Why is she here?*"

She turned to face me. "I know, I'm sorry, but Alan had already committed to staying with Jade during her mom's work trip before I even scheduled the interview. Now he's ended up in charge of both of you. It's just for a couple nights."

"*A couple nights?* With *her*? No. You are NOT doing this."

"I was going to explain everything at dinner last night but you were sound asleep and now I'm late to catch my plane and—"

"Cancel it!" I half shouted. "Right now!"

"Geo—"

Behind me, Jade was snickering. I turned to her with a sneer. "What kind of mother leaves her teenage daughter with her boyfriend, anyway? Great move. Excellent parenting. No wonder you're so messed up."

Jade stopped snickering.

"Geo, we don't have time—" said my mom desperately.

"I'll stay at Lana's," I said. "Or Feather's. Anywhere!"

She ignored all my pleas. Taking my face gently in her hands, she looked me right in the eyes. "Please. I don't ask much of you, but I'm asking now. Stay here with Alan and Jade. For me."

I squeezed my eyes shut, hating the tears that were springing to my eyes. Gently, my mom wound one of my curls behind my ear. "It's only two days."

Before I could muster another response, she glanced at her phone and took a sharp intake of breath. "Oh god the time." She gave me a tight, quick hug, then ran into the garage.

"Come on, Jade," said Alan, getting into the driver's seat as my mom climbed in the other side. "Why don't you come to the airport with us."

Alan hadn't said it like a question, but Jade took it as one anyway. "Nah," she said casually. "I'm good."

He grimaced as he put the car into reverse. "That attitude is not going to fly with me. We're going to have a serious talk when I get back."

"Can't wait!" said Jade with a snort.

I followed them out to the garage and watched the car back out in disbelief, my feet cold against the concrete driveway. My mom mouthed *I'm sorry* to me one more time, and just before pulling away, Alan leaned out and caught my eye. "Hang tight. I'll be back soon."

"Oh, don't worry about us," Jade replied, having crept up behind me like a cat stalking a mouse. "We're going to be just fine."

CHAPTER 24

Standing there under the streetlight, I watched the red taillights of Alan's Tesla glide down the street, turn at the corner, and disappear. The moment the car was out of sight, my entire brain got swallowed whole by a solitary thought: Get away.

So I did. Not caring that I was barefoot and starving, or that it was pitch-black except for the dingy orange glow coming off the streetlamp, or that I had no idea where to go, I just put one foot in front of the other and walked.

"Where do you think you're going?" Jade hiss-whispered when I reached the end of the driveway.

I didn't answer.

"I said tell me where you're going!" I heard the footsteps rushing up, but it still startled me when she grabbed my arm and spun me around. I yanked my arm back, but she was fast and grabbed my other arm, hard, her manicured nails digging into my skin. "Get back to the house. Now."

"Get off me," I said, trying to pull away. She squeezed tighter.

Well, if she thought brute force was going to work, she had another thing coming. My mom's self-defense training kicked in and, just like I'd practiced, I lashed out with my foot, jabbing her hard in the leg. I could have done a lot more damage if I'd aimed at her kneecap, but it was still a hard kick and the surprise of it made her let go.

As soon as she did, I bolted.

Jade, being a good six inches taller than me, should have been able to overtake me easily, especially since I was barefoot. Lucky for me she was wearing a pair of loose clogs and was hobbling from my kick. Plus, I'm fast. I took sharp cuts between houses and through backyards as wet grass whipped my toes and the occasional piece of gravel sent jolts up my feet. Finally, I reached the gas station and slowed down a bit, praying to gourd that I wasn't stepping in Lana's dried-up Froot Loop barf. I wasn't paying attention to where I was going, but somewhere in the middle of Main Street my lungs started burning and, feeling a cramp coming on, I slowed to a stop.

I was in front of the coffee shop, I realized. It was lit up and cozy looking and more than anything I wanted to slip inside, hide in a corner booth, and stuff myself with tea and pastries. Instead, to my horror, I heard the clomping of clogs coming from behind me. Not even stopping to look, I darted into the side alley to hide.

Instantly the shadows closed over me, so dark I couldn't see my own feet. Chest still heaving, I leaned over with my hands on my knees, staring at the end of the alley, trying to figure out what to do if she followed me in here.

I reached for my phone, thinking surely if my mom knew what was happening she'd come straight back home . . . and then cursed a very long string of every curse word I knew, plus a few extra I made up. Because of course my phone wasn't there. It was exactly where it was every night, charging on my nightstand next to my bed.

I took stock. Dark alley, no shoes, no phone, predator loose. I didn't think it could get worse until the I heard the low call of "Geeeeeoooo" coming from just around the corner.

Praying she wouldn't flick on her phone flashlight, I backed away slowly. A few steps in I turned and, setting one foot carefully in front the other, made my way deeper into the inky blackness. My hands out in front of me, I took five steps, then ten, then twenty, until finally I saw a dim, greenish light ahead.

It was now darker behind me than ahead, and when I stopped, I heard only silence. Still, I kept going, picking my way carefully toward the scrubby street behind the row of shops on Main Street. When I reached it, I paused. It smelled like porta-potty and was lit only by a couple of green security lights that cast a ghoulish tint over fire escapes, dumpsters, and dented back doors. Somehow, something told me to go left, almost like I knew where I was going.

And maybe I did.

I had only taken about ten more steps when I heard a scraping sound ahead. I froze as a soft voice called out, "Hello?"

My heart pounded as a figure stepped out of the shadows in front of me, squinting in my direction. A woman, tall and solid, holding a big black garbage bag; something about her was familiar. Cautiously, I took another step forward. That's when I registered her curly hair, freckled face, and the sweet smell of incense. "Liv?"

"Oh!" she said, dropping her bag with a plunk. "You scared me. It's Geo, right? Lana's friend?"

"That's right," I said, relief flooding every last particle of my being.

She came toward me wiping her hands on a patchwork apron. "Are you okay?" she asked, peering into my face.

"Yeah," I said, trying to swallow down the lump that was forming in my throat. "I'm good."

"Mm-hmm," she said, her mouth going crooked. "Except I can't help but notice you're alone and barefoot in a pitch-dark alley before dawn. You might want to recalibrate your idea of good?"

I glanced behind me, hoping Jade wasn't lurking in the alley somewhere, listening. To my mortification tears rose into my eyes, and I said, "Maybe not so good."

Liv's face softened and she pointed with her thumb to the door of her store. "I was just about to make breakfast and I'd love some company."

I'm pretty sure that even if I'd somehow gotten my voice to say no, my face would have said yes for me. "Thanks," I said with a sniff. "I'd like that a lot."

CHAPTER 25

I followed Liv through a back entryway into a hall stacked full of marketable woo, and it felt like walking into another dimension.

The door to the shop was at the end of the hall, its lights already on. The staircase that must have led up to Liv's apartment was just past the door. I smelled incense and sage. When I reached the doorway, I couldn't resist peeking in.

Liv noticed. "How about you stay down here and have a look around while I whip up breakfast?"

"Thanks," I said. And as she headed up the stairs, I stepped into a world of floor fountains, Buddha statues, and wind chimes.

I moseyed my way through the shop, gazing at floor-to-ceiling shelves packed with fairy figurines, tarot cards, and books on everything from reincarnation to horoscopes to nature spirit communication. As I meandered, I'm sure I looked calm, but inside my head the two sides of my mind were at war. I stopped in front of a glass cabinet featuring dark red chunks of something labeled DRAGON'S BLOOD, and the Alan side of me fired out a volley of scorn, complete with snorts and eye rolls. But the other side kept luring me forward, tantalized and curious. I would've thought I'd seen I'd seen enough woo to last me a lifetime.

Then I saw the crystal room.

No wonder Lana loved it here. There were rocks *everywhere*, with light bouncing off every sparkling surface. They were suspended from the ceiling, crowded into corners on the floor, and crammed on every shelf. They were round, square, oblong, and shaped like pyramids or animals. They were shiny and polished or rough and dull, and came in every color you could imagine, and every size, too. There was even, in the very center, a purple geode the size of a small child with a price tag so high it made me gasp.

"A beauty, isn't she?" called Liv, smiling from the doorway.

"I can't believe someone would pay this much for a giant rock," I said, knowing full well that Lana would buy it in a half a second if she could.

She smiled. "Some people believe amethyst is a powerful healing crystal."

The Alan side of my brain flared. Surely no reasonable person believed that. "You studied geophysics, right?" I asked, just to confirm.

"Yes," she said, her eyes dancing. "Did you check my credentials?"

My cheeks turned pink. "Lana might have mentioned it."

"It's okay. I know you're a skeptic," she said, laughing. "Feather told me all about it, fake fortune-telling and all."

Oh.

"You don't have to look so guilty. You're trying to help your mom. That doesn't make you a bad person; it makes you an interesting person. My favorite kind." She tilted her head toward the stairs. "Now come on up and have some pancakes. Double-frosted Oreo, my specialty."

My stomach answered for me, rumbling loud enough for both of us to hear. Liv laughed, and minutes later I found myself sitting in a green and blue kitchen that was practically glowing from the light of a rosy-pink sunrise, stuffing myself full of steaming, melty, chocolatey pancakes. I nearly groaned as I swallowed the last bite.

"I believe in putting the cake back in pancake." She grinned, licking a dollop of frosting off her spatula.

Revived by a full belly and a growing sugar buzz, I became more aware of the room I was in. "Nice place," I said. And I meant it. The whole room was as pretty and fresh as the literal daisies she'd placed in cheerful yellow vases on the table and sideboard. "My mother would love it here."

Suddenly, my heart ached at the thought of my mom in our dark, dingy kitchen with its ugly green mildew-looking walls and peeling linoleum floor that seemed dirty no matter how often she scrubbed it. I'd always insisted that Dad's house was good enough for us, no matter how old and falling apart it was. But deep down I knew it wasn't. Not for her, anyway. She deserved better.

She deserved a home like this.

And she was going to get it, I decided. One day, I was going to give it to her.

I set my chin. "I'm not going to stop."

Liv lifted her eyebrows.

"The Rock Readings," I explained. "I don't care if it's lying and cheating and wrong. I'm going to keep doing it." If I worked hard enough, we could move out of that dingy house that wasn't even ours anymore. We could move somewhere pretty and clean and bright, like this.

I figured Liv would put up some resistance to me planning to keep scamming people, but instead she led me into a sitting room as fresh and pretty as her kitchen, handed me her phone, and smiled. "I look forward to hearing more about your Rock Reading when Feather wakes up. In the meantime"—she patted the plump cushion of a green-striped sofa—"make yourself at home, and send a text to your mom and . . . who was it again?"

"Alan," I said.

"Yes, let them know you're safe. And how about you invite Lana over, too? I'm always up for another round of pancakes."

Maybe it was the softness of the plump, puffy pillows. Maybe it was the way Liv's eyes crinkled when she smiled. Or maybe she spiked the pancakes with some kind of homeopathic relaxation serum. All I know is that the moment I curled up in the corner of that fluffy couch, I felt like I was home.

CHAPTER 26

A few hours and several texts later, I was sitting at Liv's kitchen table again, salivating over the heavenly smells of my second breakfast, but this time I had Feather and Lana sitting with me.

I had been worried it would be awkward with them, given the way I'd stomped out the day before. I'd even prepared a good, long grovel, but I'd barely even started when Feather waved and said, "Forget that, that was like a thousand years ago. Why are you here *now*?" That made Lana laugh, which made me laugh, and next thing I knew we were happily snarfing more of Liv's frosted, chocolatey dessert-for-breakfast while I repeated the story of my morning.

Feather gasped in disbelief. "I can't believe that monster is at your house!"

Lana, on the other hand, was stuck on a different part of my story. "But you *can't* move to Minnesota."

"Don't worry," I said. "I'm not going anywhere."

"So you'll keep Rock Reading?" asked Feather, hopefully.

"Yup. I'm rolling with the witch thing. What do I care? It's all fake anyway."

Feather stared at me in silence for a few moments, her giant anime eyes blinking. "You *still* don't believe?"

"Oh, come on," I said, groaning. "Not this again."

Feather kept staring. "I just don't get it," she pushed. "How do you explain it all?"

"Coincidence. Plain and simple."

"But you can't possibly . . . I mean, there's no such thing as that much coincidence," sputtered Feather.

I held up my finger and quoted Alan. "Even long strings of truly bizarre coincidences are statistically inevitable."

Feather dropped back against her chair like she was completely done. Even Lana was actively sighing. I glanced at Liv and was only half surprised to see her looking at me over her shoulder with a smile dancing around her eyes.

"It's clear you like reason and science," she said, pulling off her yellow rubber gloves and draping them over the edge of the sink. "Have you ever considered the theory of alternate realities?"

"Of course." Alan and I had talked about this several times. "But there isn't any evidence for it."

Her eyes lit up even more. "You're absolutely right, there's no hard evidence at all. And yet there are physicists who find the idea of infinitely expanding realities plausible, and some who even find it probable. And if they're right, that means that every version of our lives that could possibly exist, already does, somewhere."

"They've watched too many movies is all," I said, folding my arms. "And what does that have to do with anything, anyway?"

"Wait . . ." said Feather, tapping her chin as she stared off into space for a moment. "I think I'm getting it . . ." She sat up with a gasp. "Of course! Geo's not a psychic. She's a manifester!"

Feather beamed at me like I'd just won the lottery. Even Lana leaned forward, interested. "So . . . like . . . you don't think she's predicting stuff?" she asked.

"Exactly! She's *manifesting*! She's creating a reality where the stuff she's envisioning ends up happening!" said Feather as Liv nodded, her eyes still doing their sparkly thing.

"Somebody, make it stop." I rubbed my forehead with my hand, and yet, even as I did, I felt the same curiosity I had down in Liv's shop, urging me forward. "I've heard of manifesting, but please don't tell me you think there's some sort of scientific basis for it."

Liv pulled out a chair and sat down. "Just consider, for a moment, that the theory of multiple realities is true. That everything that *could* happen *is* happening, right now, somewhere out there in the universe."

"Okay? And?"

"Now consider that what steers us through these realities is our consciousness. In other words, our thoughts and beliefs. Wouldn't it then make sense that some are gifted with the ability to surf these realities more easily than others?" She thought for a moment, looking like Feather as she tapped the table. "Or maybe think of it as being an artist. So, in the same way artists sculpt clay, or writers create stories, manifesters are creating, too. Except instead of fiction or clay, they're manipulating reality itself."

Manifesting had always seemed like something only the most gullible people would fall for. But no one had ever described it to me this way before. And as much as I wanted to roll my eyes and say something scathing, I couldn't. Because the whole time Liv had been speaking, the whispers in my mind got louder, and that now-familiar fizzy feeling was starting to shiver its way through my gut.

Feather, meanwhile, had bounced out of her chair and was twirling around the kitchen table. "I can't believe I didn't think of it right away!" she squealed as her skirt poofed around her legs. "You weren't just predicting that the snake was behind the kitty litter. You *put it* behind the kitty litter."

I glanced desperately at Lana, hoping she'd send down a rescue rope of reason. But she was just sitting there with a thousand-mile stare, nodding her head as if it was all making total sense. "It *is* an interesting theory," she said when she saw me looking at her.

"No . . ." I started, then pivoted to, "Fine. But I'd need proof."

"How much more proof could you possibly need?" Feather gushed. "You can *make things happen*! You *know* you can!" Despite my best efforts, the fizz in my gut was getting even fizzier. "I *know* you know it. I can tell. Admit it. You're feeling it."

"I . . . I really don't think—"

"Stop *thinking*," said Feather, barely stopping for a breath. "It's something you *feel*. You feel it in your heart. You're a manifester!"

Hard as I fought it, my traitorous insides were sending out wave after wave of fresh tingles. I turned to Lana again, but it seemed she'd already been swept away.

"It kind of makes sense," she was saying, her dark eyes lit as bright as Liv's. "That kitten for Alejandro? He's wanted one forever but his mom wouldn't let him have one . . . until the exact same day he talked to you. As soon as you pictured it, it happened. Doesn't that seem weird?"

"Coincidence," I sputtered, fighting the fizz with everything I had. "Listen to yourselves! You're calling me a manifester and talking about alternate realities like that makes it all scientific or something. But what you're actually talking about is *magic*."

"Exactly!" cried Feather. "It *is* magic!"

If my goal had been to reach for some logic, it backfired spectacularly. Because the moment I said that word, the fizzing inside me pushed all the way up to the top of my head, threatening to erupt like Pop Rocks in Coke.

"Hold on," cautioned Liv, holding up her hands. "Not everyone thinks it's magic. And I think we're overwhelming Geo. Let's slow this down."

"She doesn't need to slow down!" said Feather. "She's amazing! She can have anything she wants. So do it, Geo. Do it now. Whatever you want, manifest it!"

Liv said something, but I didn't hear her, because suddenly, bright as day, my mom was sitting there with all of us. I saw her as clearly as if she were really there, her head tipped back laughing, and she looked so, so happy.

A tiny last shred of me still clung to "no," but all of a sudden, totally out of my control, it was washed away by a thousand shouts of "yes!" And with that, the pressure that had been building really did feel like it exploded out the top of my head.

"Whoa!" gasped Feather, looking at Lana and Liv. "Did you feel that?"

Somehow, all four of us were now standing, looking at each other across the kitchen table like a coven of witches. Then I must've swayed because Lana grabbed my arm to steady me. "Are you okay?"

Liv rushed forward. "Sit back down and put your head on your knees."

"I'll get some water," said Feather.

"Argh!" I said, waving them off. "I'm fine. I just . . ." I looked desperately at Lana.

Her eyes softened. "Come on," she said gently, understanding what I needed better than I did. "Let's you and me go for a walk."

Without knowing quite how, I found myself down at the door to the street, wearing a pair of flip-flops and holding a bottle of water. I had never felt so strange. I wanted to cry and giggle and jump and collapse, all at the same time. Liv opened the door with a tinkle of bells, then stopped me before I walked out. "Hey, listen. I'm sorry if we overwhelmed you. These are all just theories. If any of it feels wrong to you, then it is. Period. Okay?"

I nodded. But the problem wasn't that it felt wrong.

The problem was that it felt right.

CHAPTER 27

I stepped outside and was surprised to see that the sun was still low in the sky. How was it still morning? It felt like days had passed since my mom had left. Yesterday's storm had done nothing but add heaviness to the heat, and by the time Lana and I had walked the four blocks to the park, I was sweating.

Lana seemed to sense that my words weren't working yet, so she led me quietly to the opposite side of the park from Steggy, and we plopped down in front of the biggest oak tree she could find. Collapsing back against its solid trunk, I let out a long breath and closed my eyes.

"You okay?" asked Lana, after a few peaceful minutes listening to birds sing.

"Honestly, I don't know," I said. "Feather said I should manifest something, so I pictured my mom in the room with us, and then . . . it was like everything kind of fizzed over." I lifted my head back up and took a long chug of water. "This is helping. I mostly just feel weird."

Behind me, grown-ups were pushing toddlers on baby swings. Farther off, cars zoomed by on the busy street, and we could hear the rubbery sound of a basketball thumping on the asphalt as two guys shot hoops. The ground underneath me felt comfortingly solid and real.

I took another swig of water. "So, when did you start believing in all this stuff?"

Lana sat quietly long enough that I wasn't sure she was going to answer. Then she turned toward me. "Remember Chert?"

"Of course." Chert had been Lana's dog when she was little. She didn't have her for long, but she had absolutely loved that dog.

"One day, a few weeks after she died, I took her little bed and her basket of toys to the dumpster down the street, and threw it away. It hurt too much, seeing it all the time, and I didn't want it to end up in one of my dad's piles. So I *know* her stuff wasn't in the house. Well, that night I missed her so bad I could hardly breathe." She swallowed, then continued. "And I talked to her, in my mind. I asked her to send me a sign. Something to let me know she was okay." She turned to look straight at me, her brown eyes serious. "Does that sound dumb?"

"That doesn't sound dumb at all," I said.

She nodded, not moving her eyes. "Well, that night . . . she jumped on my bed."

"She . . . what?"

"Not for real of course, but the bed shook and I felt her weight press down exactly as if she were still alive. And it wasn't scary at all. I felt okay for the first time since she died. The next morning when I woke up . . ." She paused again, then cleared her throat. "Her favorite toy was on my pillow."

Chills ran up and down my spine. "And you're *sure* you had thrown all of them away?"

"Positive. Every single one."

I chewed my lip. I knew what Alan would say. He'd have a million explanations. Like she only *thought* she threw that toy away, or her dad snuck in and put it there, or she'd been sleepwalking. He'd conveniently gloss over the fact that Lana was neat as a pin, she had never sleepwalked in her life, and her dad didn't go into her room, not for anything.

"Do you believe me?" she asked.

"I believe *you*."

"What does that mean?"

"Like, if you say it's true, then obviously I believe it happened," I said. "And it's true that I can't explain it. But all that stuff Liv and Feather said about manifesting? That goes way beyond a dog toy." I closed my eyes and listened to the soft breeze in the trees. "I don't know. It's a lot. I guess all I can do is promise that I won't close my mind to it completely."

"Not completely closed is a little bit open. That's good." Lana's face relaxed into a smile and we leaned against the tree for a while, enjoying the peace. Then she said, "This is turning out to be a weird summer."

"Understatement." I looked up into branches of green leaves patterned with sunlight and shadows. "You know who I blame?" Something small and fluttery caught my eye, floating down, swirling this way and that. It twirled and twisted until it landed right on my knee.

I picked it up and stared at it, not believing my eyes.

Lana gasped. "Feather!" She turned to me with eyes as round as Liv's pancakes. "It's a sign."

"A sign that a bird is sitting in the tree above us?"

"Geo!" she said, exasperated. "Don't ruin the moment. That was clearly a sign. Admit it."

"A sign that we're getting birdbrained?" I grinned.

"Argh!" she said, punching me in the arm. Then she stood up, tossed her braid back over her shoulder, and reached out a hand to pull me up. "Come on, Rock Reader. We've got work to do."

We made our way to Lana's house, loaded all our stuff into the red wagon, then pulled it as fast as we could to the park. We had just made it across the four-lane road when Lana stopped walking. "Whoa," she said. "That's a lot of kids."

I squinted past the swings and the guys shooting hoops on the basketball court. She was right. There was a big group of kids bunched around Steggy. More than we'd ever seen before. "We should show up late more often," I said.

But Lana was shaking her head. "It's not that, it's the videos!"

Videos? My stomach lurched. In the craziness of our morning, I had somehow managed to forget the whole stupid curse incident with Jade the day before. It felt like a million years ago. But somehow less than a day ago a bunch of kids had live streamed me threatening to curse the entire playground with a piece of lizardite. I groaned. "How bad are they?"

"Weirdly, they're not that bad. You come off a little unhinged, maybe, but in a sort of cool way. Here, look." She took out her phone, tapped an app, and held it in front of me.

Lana was being kind: I was frothing like an angry lemur performing an exorcism. Nothing about me in that video was cool. But the main thing I noticed was that it had *tons* of views. Sure, most of the comments were nasty, but so what? The ones with the most engagement of all were from the Jackson sisters, who had come out to support me in force. Good ole Zafirah. She'd stayed true to her word, and then some.

"Lana, this is perfect. No wonder there's a crowd!"

Underneath my glee, though, was a big bunch of nerves. I'd beaten Jade, and she wasn't going to forget it. No wonder she'd been so nasty to me earlier. It didn't make me look forward to going home again.

Luckily, I didn't need to think about that yet. We heard a "Hey!" coming from across the park and saw a skinny girl with a pointy chin heading our way. She looked young, maybe eight years old, but she marched toward us with her head high and haughty, like a teacher handing out a discipline slip. "Hey," she said again, sharply. "Are you coming or what? Because I need a witch."

CHAPTER 28

Despite my worry about Jade, I laughed. "Sure thing, just let us get set up first." Lana and I pulled the wagon together, and when we got close enough to the crowd I called out, "Line up by the dinosaur, please. We'll be ready in five."

Lana got to work setting up the table and placing her rocks in rows, while I focused on the easel. When I grabbed the giant pad of paper, I realized that Manuel's witch drawing was still the top page, and paused. Maybe I wasn't a witch, exactly, but Liv, Feather, and Lana sure seemed to think I was a manifester, and that was pretty close.

I could use it.

I pulled Lana aside for a quick business discussion, and, after figuring out the details, I flipped Manuel's drawing over. On the fresh page, in giant neon letters, I wrote:

THE ROCK READERS
WE DON'T JUST PREDICT YOUR FUTURE.
WE MANIFEST IT.
$20
WE MAKE DREAMS COME TRUE!
MONEY-BACK GUARANTEE

There was plenty of grumbling when everyone saw the new price, but I reassured them that the new rate wouldn't go into effect until the next day. Besides, I told them, we were worth it.

"We literally make wishes come true. We're basically fairy godmothers with rocks. That's worth way more than twenty dollars." Some people still looked skeptical, and I could hardly blame them. But I didn't show an ounce of my own doubt. If I could make them believe even just a tiny bit, we'd pull in more money than ever.

We were unfolding our chairs when Feather and her umbrella bobbed into view. "Ooh, I love it!" she said when she saw the new poster.

Before I could reply, the small girl with the pointy chin stepped forward. "Hey. Remember me? Your *customer*? Who's been *waiting*?" She thrust out a ten, and sat down like she owned the place.

"Wow," I said, taking the bill and handing it to Lana. "Aggressive."

"No fair!" shouted two kids who'd been shoving each other at the head of the line. "We were here first!"

"Only because they saw me coming and ran ahead," said the girl, squaring her bony butt stubbornly on the chair.

"Chill, all of you. Everyone will get a turn." I turned back to the girl. "You, pick two rocks, and tell me your wish."

She snatched up a white rock that looked exactly like marble, but which I remembered from Lana's notes was a mineral called howlite. Her second choice was a thin, layered silvery rock that sparkled when it caught the sun. "Mica?" I asked in a whisper. Lana nodded.

My young, very pushy customer, plunked them down in front of me with a bang. "I want to be a K-pop star."

I blinked. Not only was this kid way too young to be any kind of star, she looked about as white as it got. "A Korean pop star?" I clarified, hoping I'd somehow heard wrong.

"That's right," she said, with a confidence I could almost admire.

"Ummmm, yeah. I don't think that's going to happen."

She crossed her arms. "Why not?"

"Because . . . wait. Are you Korean?"

"No. So what? I paid," she said, pointing a sharp finger at the sign. For a kid who could fit in a packet of gum, she sure had big attitude. "It says right there you make dreams come true. So do it."

It hit me that I probably should have learned a little more about this manifesting stuff before branding myself as an expert. What was I supposed to do when someone asked for something completely unrealistic? I shot a desperate look at Feather.

"A manifester can only manifest things they can believe in," she said in a soft voice. "If Geo doesn't believe something is possible, she won't be able to picture it clearly, and it won't work." I nodded like I'd been about to say the same thing.

"This is a rip-off," said the pint-sized girl, folding her arms. "I want my money back."

I closed my eyes and took a deep breath. When I opened them, I asked, "What's your name?"

"Nina."

"And you're what, eight?"

"Ten," she said, puffing up. "I'm petite."

"Okay, so what does a petite ten-year-old such as yourself want to be a K-pop star for anyway? Sure, they're famous, but aren't most of them miserable?"

Nina continued glaring. "You don't know that."

I sighed. "Fine. I'll tune in and see what the rocks say. Who knows? Maybe they really can perform miracles." Lana and I did our usual whispering as she explained the rocks to me. Before she'd even finished, an image of Nina popped into my mind, standing in a circle of light wearing a soft pink skirt and ballet slippers. She was doing pliés and pirouettes and wasn't half bad. Her pointy chin looked kind of cute with her strawberry hair pulled up in a bun and all the glittery stage makeup on.

I turned back to Nina. "Do you dance ballet?"

Her eyes widened with surprise. "I did until last month. Did someone tell you that?"

"The rocks told me," I said, glad my hunch was right. "And that's your real dream, isn't it? To be a ballet dancer."

She shifted uncomfortably as her eyes darted toward the crowd of kids. "No."

I didn't know why she was lying, but she was. I was sure of it.

"Look, if you don't listen to me, listen to the rocks. See how shiny this mica is? It's a good omen. It means you're going to shine. But the howlite's message is even more important because it's telling you that you can't shine by trying to be something you're not. People try to pass howlite off as turquoise all the time by dyeing it. And it might fool some people, but mostly all it does is ruin a perfectly good rock. That shiny, glittery, sparkly life you want? It'll happen if you stick with ballet."

I sat back, feeling pretty good about myself. But the girl stood up, jutted out her hand, and said, "Give me my money back."

I blinked. "You took up my time, you got your reading, and on top of that some really good advice, and you want your money back?"

She stomped her very petite foot. "You didn't give me my wish."

"I *did* give you your wish. Your *real* wish. Deep down you don't even want to be a pop star!"

She twirled toward the crowd. "She's lying. She's a cheat!"

Heat rose in my cheeks and the image of her dancing came into my mind again, only this time it was on fire. I gleefully watched her twirly pink skirt smoke and burn, until something icy flashed through me, snapping me back to the real world.

I shook my head to clear the image. "Okay, here's the deal. We can return your money and never give you another reading again. Ever. OR you can accept that you got a fair deal and maybe one day we'll allow you to come back."

The girl weighed my words for a moment, then pulled her hand back with a huff. "Fine." She executed a perfect ballerina pirouette and glided off.

"Dang," I said, wiping my forehead with my T-shirt sleeve. I gestured for Lana and Feather to lean in close. "I genuinely wanted to torch that kid," I whispered to Feather. "Is that bad?"

Feather looked at me sideways. "Does that happen often?"

"She definitely has a temper," said Lana.

I squirmed. If I didn't really believe in all this, why was I worried? Even so, I needed to know. "Could I hurt someone that way?"

Her face went deadly serious. "Have bad things happened to your enemies in the past? Spontaneous combustion? Demon possession? Rare, deadly diseases?"

"No! Please tell me you're joking!"

"Yeah," she said, breaking into a grin. "Totally kidding. You're fine. I mean, never manifest anything bad on purpose, obviously. Definitely no extended revenge fantasies. That would be, like, super dark, and it would also boomerang back on you, so be careful. But now that you know you're a manifester you'll be fine, because you'll stop yourself."

"I wouldn't be so sure," cut in Lana with a grimace. "Can you?"

"Hey!" I protested. "Of course I can." Then I paused. "But what if I can't?"

"Okay," said Feather, "so let's say you get mad and start picturing something scary. There's an easy fix for that. As soon as you notice, just say 'cancel, clear, delete.'"

"That's it?" I asked.

"Yup," she said. "Works every time."

Next to me, I could feel Lana relax.

"Do I have to say it out loud?" I asked.

"Nope. In your head is fine," said Feather. "But you do have to mean it."

Cancel, clear, delete, I thought, picturing Nina's burning skirt. The image reverted to one of her dancing in the spotlight and I felt immediately relieved.

"Thanks," I said, exhaling. I glanced back at the line of kids, which had grown longer since we'd sat down. "Better get back to work."

"That reminds me . . ." Feather opened her giant patchwork tote and pulled out several peaches, a bag of trail mix, and some frosty boxes of frozen lemonade. "From Aunt Liv. She said manifesting can mess with your blood sugar."

My stomach rumbled just looking at it. "Thanks!" I said, before biting into a peach so juicy it dribbled down my chin.

I turned back to my line and called out with my mouth full, "Next!"

CHAPTER 29

The rest of the readings that day were pretty uneventful. We had a few kids who wanted their baseball or Ultimate Frisbee team to win, another handful who wanted to master their favorite video game. One wanted a guinea pig, another one wanted a pony, another a T-rex. I told the first one I was getting him two guinea pigs, not one, because piggies need friends. I told the other kid I might not manage to get her a pony of her own, but I could definitely manage some riding lessons. And the last one I explained I could only get her a bunch of T-rex stuffies and figurines, not the real thing, which thankfully she was okay with.

And those were just the little kids. We also had a bunch more high school kids stop by. Five senior girls came in a clump and asked to share the fee if I could get them all into the same college together. I charged them a cool fifty and let them choose their rocks as a group. At the end of the day Feather busied herself folding up the chairs as I packed the easel and Lana sorted rocks. She paused, flint in hand. "Jade never showed up."

"I know," I said, eyeing the flint. "It's weird. I don't like it. Has she posted anything yet today?"

Lana scrolled through her phone for a bit. "Not that I can see."

"That's even weirder."

"I wish you didn't have to go back to your house," said Feather.

"Me too," I said. "But I'm going to have to face her sooner or later. Besides, it's not like I'm scared of her." I puffed myself up. "If anything, she should be scared of me."

By the time I got home I was as tired as a limp dollar bill and tense as a guitar string, all at the same time. It was not a good feeling. I tugged open the squeaky screen door and the house, thank gourd, seemed quiet and empty. So I trudged my way upstairs, set Fridgie to high, and fell on my bed, soaking in the relief of finally having my phone back.

It had been less than twenty-four hours since I'd last checked my phone messages, but it felt like days. Sure enough, I had about a bazillion messages. Most were from my mom.

"Miss you already Slime Trail," the first one said.

Then, "Made it safe to the airport. You good?"

Then, "In MN. Would you guess it's even hotter here? Also, there are mosquitoes."

Then, "Check this out!" sent with a random picture of a giant cherry-on-a-spoon sculpture.

There were a bunch more like those, then the last one said, "Heading into first interviews, wish me luck. Txt when you get back to your phone."

"Jade stinks worse than donkey cheese," I texted. Moments later my phone rang.

There was a long happy squeal when I picked up. "You're there! Finally!"

I knew I should ask her how her interviews were going, but the truth was I didn't want to hear about it. So I gave her all the details on my morning instead. When I finished, there was a short silence. "So you really kicked her? And then ran away? And that's why you didn't have your phone all day?"

"Hey, don't make it sound like I did something wrong. Jade's the bad guy, remember?"

"Sorry, Skid Mark," she said. "It just scared me having you out of touch that long. Don't go out without your phone again, okay?" I was about to defend myself when she said, "Shoot, I've got to hang up soon and I haven't heard about the rest of your day. Tell me quick, starting with when you left your friend's place. What's their shop called again? Incense and Sensibility? Great name."

"Well, so Lana and I did more Rock Readings, except..."

I hesitated. It sounded embarrassing enough in my head, but I knew it would sound a thousand times worse out loud. My mom waited.

"Okay," I started again, "so you know how a lot of my predictions have been coming true? Alan says it's coincidence, and obviously that's the rational thing to believe. But Feather and her aunt Liv think it's me. That I'm... making stuff happen." I winced.

"Okay," said my mom, drawing it out like she wanted to hear more.

"It sounds really dumb, but it's called manifesting," I said, flushing with embarrassment as I said it. "So, like, when I picture stuff happening, it happens."

"Yes," she said. "I've heard of manifesting."

When she didn't say more, I got impatient. "So what do you think? I mean, it's ridiculous, isn't it?"

"I don't know. What do you think?"

"Ugh!" Sometimes my mom is so determined for me to make my own decisions, she fails to ever tell me what she thinks herself. "Seriously, Mom. It's freaking me out and I need a straight answer: Do you think it's possible? Could this whole stupid manifesting thing be real?"

"I'm not sure anything is impossible," she said vaguely.

"So that's a yes."

"Not necessarily," she said. Maddening! "I'm just not sure this sort of thing is ever really knowable."

"Fine," I huffed. "Then how about signs? Do you think it's possible to get a sign from the universe? Like a feather landing on your knee, or a dead dog leaving a chew toy on your bed?"

"Those are pretty specific examples." She laughed. "But if it means something to the person who receives it, then does it matter if it's real or not?"

What kind of a question was that? "Of course it does!"

"I'm not so sure," she replied. "I think sometimes a thing can be true and not true, all at the same time. Or maybe by believing it, we make it true. Ultimately, it's what we bring to it that matters, and what it brings to us."

"That makes no sense!" In a thousand years I would never get a straight answer out of her. "You'll at least admit that Dad would say it was totally pathetic, right? To even be considering it?"

There was a long pause. "Not necessarily."

"Oh, come on," I said. "Now you're just saying whatever."

"I swear I'm not," she said. "In college, yes, your dad would have scoffed at this entire conversation. But if he were alive today? I don't know. People change. Sometimes a lot. He died so young, it's impossible to guess what he would think now."

"But Alan was just like him, and he hasn't changed at all."

My mom had a fast answer to that. "Don't mix Alan up with your father. They might have thought alike back then, but they were always very different people."

I felt surprise like an exclamation point in my mind. "Different how?"

"It's hard to put into words. . . . Your dad was so much like you, all fire and flame. He'd flare up, full of conviction, then the next instant he'd move on, burning bright about something else. Alan was more like the fuel that kept the fire burning. Or, no, maybe more like a steady wind, always blowing from the same direction. For the years they were friends, Alan fanned and fueled your father's skepticism. But there's no guessing what your father would think now."

I sat with this a while.

"I'm sorry, Cactus Breath, my next interview is coming up. I wish I could talk longer."

"Me too," I said.

"You're going to be okay?"

"Of course," I said.

Her reply was soft. "Over and over again, you amaze me. Love you, Butter Brain."

But I hardly heard her as I turned off my phone. In my mind, something interesting was happening. Alan and my dad were separating like a dividing cell. My whole life I'd cared so much what Alan thought because he and my dad had seemed almost like a single organism, with the same thoughts, the same beliefs, and the same outlook. Suddenly, they were distinct. Maybe Alan would judge me for believing in non-provable things, but what if my dad didn't? What if he'd changed his mind, like my mom said?

If only I could just ask him.

Then again . . . maybe I could.

CHAPTER 30

I swung my legs over the edge of my bed, rested my elbows on my knees, and covered my eyes with my palms. This entire crazy week only happened because I'd asked my dad for help. Couldn't that mean he might be out there, watching over me? Listening? Wanting to help some more?

The thought made my heart beat quicker. "Dad?" I asked. "You here? Can we talk?"

Nothing happened.

Something was missing. Feather was sure I was a medium, and that kid's dead grandpa sure seemed to agree. That had happened during a Rock Reading. Did I need to pick out some rocks to talk to my dad? Thanks to Lana, I had bunches of them all around my room. I closed my eyes. "Hey, Dad, want to pick some rocks?"

I gave it a few seconds, then got up from my bed and wandered around my room to see if anything jumped out at me. When I got to my closet, I rummaged through first one shelf, then the next, until I saw it. It was right there in front of my blue money box, a small, blue-green tumbled crystal covered in shimmery, feathery white lines, and somehow I just knew it was the one. What had Lana told me this was? When it came to me, my insides went all fluttery. *Seraphinite*, she'd said. Seraphinite, as in another word for angels. What was my dad, if not my guardian angel?

The next rock took a bit longer to find. I gathered them up from every hiding spot I could think of, but nothing felt quite right until I found a little reddish-brown rock that had fallen behind my desk and was half hiding in dust bunnies. If you didn't know better, you'd think it was nothing but a worthless piece of gravel. You'd be very wrong. This, I knew, was zircon, which was one of Lana's favorites because when it's cut and polished like a gemstone, it's the only rock more brilliant than diamond. In rock terms that means how much light bounces off its surfaces, giving it that sparkle that jewelry people love. But I knew Lana thought it could mean brilliance in the smart sense of the word, too, and she carried one for good luck anytime she had a test. I guess it works, because that girl aces everything.

Anyway, my brilliant, smart dad was exactly who I needed, and even without that, zircon just felt like the right choice. So

I closed my eyes, cupped both rocks to my chest, and called out to him in the dark and quiet of my mind.

At first, nothing happened.

"Dad?" I called again into the emptiness. For good measure, I added, "Paging Joey Leoni. Your daughter needs to talk to you, like, right now please."

And then, with a noise like a spotlight turning on, he appeared, standing on a stage under a bright circle of light.

With a beard.

"Seriously?" I asked. "Facial hair?" In no video or photo I'd ever seen of him had he ever been anything but clean shaven. The dad in my imagination laughed, and instantly, the beard was gone. His eyes were wrinkled beneath his rectangle glasses, and his hair, still light, was more gray than blond.

"So people age in heaven?" I asked him. "Or . . . wherever you are. Where exactly are you?"

"In your mind, of course," he said. "And I thought the beard lent me a certain air of maturity and wisdom."

"Um . . . no," I said, laughing. "Trust me, you are not a beard guy. Anyway, we need to talk. Crazy things are happening lately and I need to know if I'm nuts to believe in any of it."

"Nuts? Well, that's a good start. They're brain food. Walnuts, especially. They even resemble little brains—"

"Dad!" I cut in, like he'd been cracking dad jokes my whole life. "Come on, I meant *me*. Am I nuts?"

"What, just because you're sitting alone on your bed talking with an imagined version of your long-dead father? What could be nuts about that?"

"BE SERIOUS." I would never have guessed that my dad was such a doofus. He always seemed so fierce and intimidating speaking from podiums in the videos. "Tell me if what's happening to me is real. Like you, for starters. Are you actually here, or is it purely imagination? Like, am I connecting to the real you, or just something my mind is creating?"

"What does your gut tell you?"

Ugh. That was exactly the kind of thing my mom would ask. I pictured myself crossing my arms. "I don't speak gut."

He gave me a look. A very dad look. "Try anyway."

Fine. I turned my thoughts to focusing on how my body felt. The first thing I noticed was my heart was pounding and I was barely breathing. But underneath that, the fizz was starting to bubble and froth. I did my best to translate the feelings into words. "I think . . . my gut *wants* this to be real?" As soon as I said it, I clenched. "But it also doesn't want to feel like an idiot. I mean, we're talking about magic here."

He beamed. "See? You do speak gut."

"Yes, but all it told me is what I want. That doesn't help at all."

"I disagree. Knowing what you want is at least half the equation."

"Then what's the rest?"

"Deciding."

I took this in and chewed on it for a while, then gave up in frustration. "If I wanted vague answers, I would've asked Mom. You're either real, or you're not real. You're here, or I'm making you up. Period."

"You are making me up. That doesn't mean I'm not real."

I huffed in frustration. "Quit with the wizard riddles! I need to know if I can trust all this woo-garbage, or if I'm making a jerk of myself. Give me answers. Talk straight."

He nodded. "Okay, so here's the deal: I'm saying that *you* get to decide which world you live in. A world with magic, or a world without. One isn't more true than the other. It's just a choice."

"Then why are you dead? Because if I get to choose what world I live in, then I want to live in the world where you're still here. I want you to be alive again."

He squeezed his eyes shut. "I'm sorry, kiddo. I may have overstated things. If you choose a world with magic, you can make stuff happen, but there are limits. It's real magic, not fantasy."

"Hmph," I said. "That probably means I can't fly either."

He held up his fingers and started ticking off. "No flying. No teleportation. No bringing back the dead. No walking on water. Basically no Harry Potter or biblical-level stuff. Though you might be able to work up a decent locust plague."

I laughed despite myself. "All right, so basically I can do nothing cool unless it involves a bunch of nasty flying bugs."

"Untrue. You can do incredible things. Take this. Us, talking. Isn't that something?"

I blinked. Yes, it was. Definitely. If it was real, and not just me creating a giant wish-fulfilling fantasy. My doubts roared back. After all, why should I trust this imaginary version of my dad? He sure didn't sound like the dad I knew from videos. He sounded like the dad I wanted to hear. If I was going to believe in something so nuts, I needed more. Suddenly, I sat up straight.

"I need a sign. Like, a really stupidly obvious one. Then I'll know for sure."

He sighed. "Because the video and the feather and the dozens of successful manifestations weren't enough?"

"Extraordinary claims require extraordinary evidence," I said in my best Alan voice. "Just send me one more sign, then I'm in. But it has to be unmistakable."

"Fine." He grinned. "But you don't need me for that. Do it yourself."

"How do I—" Even as I asked the question, I was already picturing myself fully convinced, a true believer. And that's when I finally admitted it to myself: I did want it. Not just being able to talk my dad, but all of it. The magic, the manifesting, the weirdness, and the woo. It was strange and a little scary, and part of me was still resisting, but there it was.

I was officially moving over to the Feather side of life.

"See? I told you that you could do it yourself," my dad said. Then he reached up, grabbed the string of the light bulb hanging over the stage, and pulled.

The stage went dark and quiet. "Thanks, Dad," I said into the emptiness. My throat tightened. "I miss you."

I opened my eyes. "Well," I said to my empty room. "That was different."

Underneath Fridgie's whirring, everything was normal and still, if a little bright. I sat up and wiped my eyes on my sleeve. "All right, Dad," I said to the air with a smile. "I'll be waiting on that sign."

Immediately, as if in response, the door to my bedroom flew open.

CHAPTER 31

Sadly, the door flying open was not my sign. If anything, it was my anti-sign.

It was Jade.

"Hello? Knock?"

She ignored me, leaning into my room, scanning it wall to wall.

"What do you want?" I asked, my hostility rising.

Jade snapped her eyes back to me, broke into a sudden, dazzling smile, and said, "Dinner!" Then, with a graceful spin, she began to descend the stairs. I trusted that smile not one little bit. I'd have felt safer if she'd chewed me out.

Stepping as if she might have booby-trapped my staircase, I made my way to the kitchen, my nose wrinkling more the closer I got.

"What's that smell?"

"Salmon!" said Alan, busy at the stove. He was wearing the frilly, flowery apron my mom had gotten as a joke around his waist.

Jade perched on the end of her chair and gave Alan a look of adoration so fake it would have fooled no one except Alan himself. "It was my special request," she said.

"It's my mom's recipe," Alan continued, flushing with pleasure. "I'm surprised I've never made it for you before . . ." His voice trailed off, then he turned. "Oh no. You hate fish! I knew you hated fish. How could I have forgotten?" He smacked his forehead, sending a smattering of grease spittle onto the counter behind him.

"Gosh, what a coincidence!" Jade said with a comically evil grin. Chills crept up my spine. How on earth did Jade Sinclair know that I hate fish? Or was it really a coincidence? But then, wasn't it a coincidence that she was bringing up coincidence?

Everything about this conversation was giving me heebie-jeebies.

"I don't mind," I said, forcing a smile. "It smells sort of good." He instantly relaxed. Poor old Alan. How could someone who prided himself on skepticism be so easy to fool?

"Okay, phew!" he said, handing me a plate of nasty pink fish flesh. I covered it with a heaping pile of rice, then took the chair opposite Jade.

"So, Alan," said Jade, her eyes fluttering between us, "did Geo tell you she's still doing her little witch stand?"

"Ah, I figured you'd keep at it," he said. "How's it going?"

"It's . . ." I paused as my cheeks reddened. Now that I was more open to it, talking about the woo in front of Alan had gotten more complicated. "It's good."

"Come now," cut in Jade. "It's not just good. Everyone is talking about you."

"Yes, and thank you for that," I said, picking up my fork. "Genius marketing you gave us."

Alan looked back and forth, correctly sensing danger. "Girls—"

"Here's what I want to know," said Jade, talking right over him. "We both know you were faking it when you started. But you're not anymore, are you? You think it's real."

My stomach dropped. It was like she knew how badly I wouldn't want to talk about it in front of Alan. So, naturally, she was trying to force me into doing exactly that.

I wasn't about to let her corner me. I took a bite and said, "Whatever. You're the one who convinced everyone I'm real."

She narrowed her eyes. "Why won't you just say it?"

"Why do you care?" I snapped.

"Girls!" said Alan. "Stop this right now, both of you. Jade, trust me, Geo would never fall for her own con. She's far too smart for that."

She flicked a wave of hair over her shoulder and said, "Are you sure, though? Why don't you ask her? Right now?"

Thankfully, Alan didn't ask. He just sighed and gave me a sympathetic *I'm-sorry* look. Then he wiped his mouth with one of my mom's neatly pressed cloth napkins and said, "If Geo believed she could make things happen, surely she'd have tried to win the lottery by now." He shot me a wink. "The PowerMillions drawing is tomorrow night. Fifty-five million. You win that and I'll proclaim you magical myself."

Alan cheerfully veered off into the statistics of lotteries, complete with a list of things more likely than winning one, like being struck by lightning, having a vending machine fall on you, or getting eaten by a shark. Or getting struck by lightning while being eaten by a shark after they've tossed you into the ocean for wrecking the vending machine.

But I only dimly heard him. I also didn't notice Jade watching me as she ate.

How could I have? My thoughts were running a mile a minute as fizz bubbled through my body, filling my ears with static. Alan had offered up the answer. Winning that PowerMillions wouldn't just prove manifesting was real, it would solve every problem we had, and then some. This *had* to be my dad's sign. He said I could choose magic, so I would.

I'd choose it in my heart, I'd choose it in my soul, I'd choose it in my bones.

Nothing was going to keep me from making those millions mine.

CHAPTER 32

I barely remember the rest of that night. I finished the meal and got ready for bed like I was walking through a dream. Maybe Lana's brilliant zircon had rubbed off on me, because I worked out the entire lottery plan in no time at all, and if I do say so myself, it was brilliant.

The sound of the coffee grinder and pans clanking against the stove woke me out of happy million-dollar dreams, and I stared up at my ceiling savoring the feeling until the smell of bacon drifted into my room, making my stomach grumble. Buzzing with the knowledge that this was the day my entire life was going to change, I reached over for my phone on my nightstand table to check the time.

It was gone.

I froze, my hand hanging in the air, trying to process the blank space where my phone should be. My phone was never gone. It was always there. *Always.*

Then my breath caught. Because of course: Jade. I knew she was a snake, and now she'd struck.

I yanked on my shorts, slipped on my sandals, and flung open my door, ready to battle. My anger got hotter with every step I took down the creaky old steps, and by the time I reached the kitchen, I was steaming like a Yellowstone geyser.

"She took my phone."

Alan turned from the stove, the frilly retro apron puffing out over his skinny hips and chest, and waved a pair of greasy tongs at me. "Good morning! You're just in time for some Ruffly Fluffly Bubbly."

"My *phone*, Alan. She *took* it."

His face went from cheerful to alert. "Who, Jade?"

"No, Cookie Monster. Who do you think? She crept into my *room* last night, and she took it."

"Now, come on, that's a pretty big accusation. Are you sure it didn't fall under the bed?"

I snorted in exasperation. "She took it, and I'm getting it back."

"Geo, wait!" he called, springing after me. "Stop. Let's talk about this."

I did stop, but only because there in the hall, slithering toward me with a delighted smile, was Jade.

"Good morning!" she said, breezing past me and grabbing a strip of bacon from the plate by the stove.

I stomped toward her, but Alan put himself between us, stretching out his hands like he could hold us in place with a Jedi force field.

"Jade," he said, trying to sound calm. "Geo's phone seems to be missing. I don't suppose you could shed any light on that?"

"Me?" she said, fluttering her hand to her heart. "No, I haven't seen it anywhere!"

I practically snarled.

Alan lifted his arm higher. "Geo—"

"Don't Geo me! I *know* she took it, Alan."

When he said my name again, he said it with a sharpness he'd never used on me before. "Innocent until proven guilty. Now, look. I'm sure if you give it time, it'll pop up."

I stared from Jade's cold, smug face back to his pleading one. I could hardly believe what I was hearing. He was taking *her* side? The injustice, the unfairness, and the humiliation of it all took my breath away. Suddenly, to my horror, I realized there were tears in my eyes.

No way was I going to let Jade see me fall apart. So I turned on my heels, and I ran.

I was mortified to cross the park in a full-on rage cry. Swiping my cheeks with my arm, I realized I was nowhere near ready to interact with other humans. So instead of heading toward Steggy, I went and found the old, giant oak tree Lana and I had sat under the day before, and sank down with my back against its scratchy trunk to let myself have a good, angry, hot-tears kind of cry. Once I was finished, everything seemed sharper, the way colors seem sharper after a storm.

Why was I crying over Alan and stupid Jade, anyway? And what did it matter if she stole my phone? I was about to have so much money I could buy a thousand new ones. Even Alan would admit I was a manifester once I won that lottery. All I had to do was get the ticket. The rest would happen like magic.

I stood up, ready to find Lana. But before I took a step, I saw something flutter by in the corner of my eye. I stooped to the grass and picked it up.

Another white feather.

I squinted up at the old, gnarled branches and summer-green leaves. "Well, Dad," I said. "Either a hawk left its kill up there, or you really love sending me feathers. But, just so you know, I'd love an even bigger sign. I promise I'll stop asking after today. It's just that Feather said I can only manifest things

I truly believe are possible. And I *do* think I can do this . . . but one more unmistakable sign from you would help even more."

Hoping that was enough, I put the feather carefully in my pocket, took a deep breath, and headed for Steggy.

CHAPTER 33

As I made my way from one end of the park to the other, my senses were so pricked up I noticed everything, from the branches blowing in the breeze to the sound of the cars going by and a basketball bouncing. When I passed a mom struggling to get her toddler into a baby swing, the kid looked right at me and said, "Feather!"

Whoa.

"That's not me, bud, that's my friend." Usually I found little kids annoying, but something about this one, with his white blond hair and blue eyes staring like he already knew me, was hard to resist.

He pointed again, his little chubby arm stretched to its limit. "Feather!"

The mom smiled sheepishly as she shifted him to her hip. "Sorry. He's got a bit of an obsession with feathers."

"With *feathers*?" I repeated.

She laughed. "It's a little random, I know. He collects them."

Um, yes, that was random. And definitely a coincidence, if coincidences were something you believe in, which I no longer did.

On impulse, I reached into my pocket and pulled out the white feather. "Here you go, buddy," I said, holding it out to him. "For your collection."

He squealed with delight and squirmed until his mom put him down. He balled his fist around the feather and looked at me with his eyes all lit up. "Feather!"

"Exactly," I said. "And wow have I got a friend you need to meet."

"Aww, very pretty," said his mom. "Say thank you, Joey."

"Tank you!" he said.

Wait. His name was Joey? The same name as my dad? That was weird. "Um, it was nice to meet you, Joey."

"Bye, Deo!" The world dimmed. Did he just call me Geo?

"I'm sorry," I said to his mom. "Have we met before?"

"Oh, no, we just moved here," said his mom. "Me, Joey, and—" She glanced around. "There. His big sister, Amber. She's nine."

A girl with shiny auburn hair was running toward us, but she wasn't alone: Right on her heels was Mei, my very first client.

"That's her! The girl I told you about!" panted Mei, pointing at me.

The red-haired girl squealed, then turned to her mom breathlessly. "Mom, remember I told you at dinner last night how Mei picked the amber and the Rock Reader told Mei she'd meet a new best friend in the park and she'd be a girl with amber hair?" She breathed it all like a single word, then turned to me. "You were right! Except I don't just have amber hair. Even my *name* is Amber!"

I felt dizzy.

The mom looked at me kind of funny. "Wow. You sound like the real deal."

Amber jumped up and down. "Can I have a reading, Mom? I want one. It's twenty dollars, please?"

"I think I'd like one myself." The mom laughed.

"Me!" said Joey. "Me!"

"Yes, Joey, you can have a reading too. Maybe another day." She turned back to me. "This explains why Joey was drawn to you. He's kind of the real deal himself. He probably sensed a kindred spirit."

"So . . ." I said. "You believe in all this, then?" I waved my fingers around. "Like, spirits and signs and stuff?"

"Of course. Runs in the family. Skipped me, sadly, but my grandmother had the gift, and Joey does for sure."

"Wow," I said, my head swimming as I pointed vaguely toward Steggy. "Well, come anytime, we're over by the yellow dinosaur."

"Perfect," she said. "We'll see you soon." She pulled Joey back toward the swings. "All right, little guy. Say goodbye."

"Bye, Deo!" he said, waving his feather in his fist.

My breath caught as chills spread up my arms. "Hold up a sec," I said. "Did Mei or Amber tell you my name?"

"No." Joey's mom looked confused for a moment. "I'm sorry, that was rude of me. I should've asked."

"No, it's not that," I explained. "It's just . . ." I glanced at Joey. "I think he was saying my name. Geo. That's me."

"Ahh, I see." She didn't seem surprised at all. "Well, there's no doubt about it, then. You two have a connection, for sure."

What could I do but agree? Not only did Joey know my name, but he shared the same name as my dad, he came from a family of psychic woo believers, and, on top of that, another one of my predictions had come weirdly, wildly, ridiculously true. I felt myself fill up with so much fizz I practically floated across the park. And this time, not one tiny part of me tried to fight it.

CHAPTER 34

When I finally reached Steggy, I was surprised to find not only Lana waiting for me, but Feather, too. This was the first time she'd shown up for breakfast on the bench. That had always been just me and Lana, yet somehow, I didn't mind her being there. It was weirdly nice seeing her face light up when she saw me.

Lana's face, however, did not light up. If anything, she straight-up glared. "Why have you been ignoring my texts?"

"It's not my fault!" I said, holding up my hands. "Jade stole my phone!" I patted my pockets, proving their emptiness.

That made the glare fall right off her face. "She *what*?"

"Yeah, for real. But I don't even care. I don't care about her anymore, or my phone, or anything, because listen to this." I rapid-fire explained about talking to my dad, the lottery idea he gave me, and then the extra-huge bonus sign of meeting

Joey. I was bouncing around Feather-style as I spoke, and had expected them to get excited, too. But that's not what happened.

I trailed off awkwardly. "What's wrong?"

"The lottery?" asked Lana pointedly.

Instantly, a rush of guilt swelled up. Because, duh, of course Lana would hate this plan. She loathed lotteries, had always loathed them, and with good reason. Her dad bought a ticket a day at least. And when he didn't win (which, of course, was always), he'd toss them down wherever he happened to be standing, all over the piles in their house. She despised those little white scraps of paper. She called them hoarder confetti.

I swallowed. "I'm a terrible person. I should've remembered." It sounded exactly as lame as it was.

"You're not terrible," she said, before sighing. "But I'm not going to stop you, am I?"

Desperate for backup, I turned to Feather. But she looked as deflated as a leftover birthday balloon.

"Sorry," she said, looking genuinely pained. "It's just . . ." She bit her lip for a second before plunging forward. "Manifesting lotteries doesn't work. Like, hardly ever. Liv says it's because you can't control the how. Like . . . you can manifest being rich, for sure. That's the what. But how it happens? You have to leave that to the universe. The lottery is a how."

What the dunk was she talking about? I did *not* want to hear this. Not any of it. Not now.

She tugged on a wisp of her hair, then continued. "So, like, if I wanted to manifest a trip to Scotland, I wouldn't focus on the airplane flight, right? That's the how. You have to let the universe figure that stuff out. Instead, I'd go straight to picturing the lochs, the bagpipes, the foggy mornings, the old crumbling castles..." A dreamy look came over her as she got lost in the visions of her mystical vacation.

"That's totally different," I said, yanking her out of it. My voice came out louder than I meant it to be. "The lottery *is* the what. I asked my dad to help, and five minutes later Alan told me about the PowerMillions drawing. It was a sign. I *know* it was a sign."

"I thought Joey was your sign?" Feather asked.

"They were both signs!" *Yeesh!* Since when was Feather the one with doubts? I tried to keep my voice calm. "Okay, listen. Both of you. Lana, I'm really sorry. But trust me, this time it's different. This is going to solve all of our problems, *all* of them, and I *know* I can do it." I turned to Feather. "Can't you feel the energy?"

I heard what I'd said, and snapped my mouth shut. Me, trying to convince Feather to feel the energy? Alan would think I'd lost my mind.

But then I shook the thought away and kept going, because I knew I was right. "Look, even if you both hate it, tickets are only a dollar. One freaking dollar! Please. Say yes. For me."

"It *is* only a dollar," said Feather, looking at Lana. "And it's not like anything bad will happen if she tries, except being disappointed."

"We won't be disappointed!" I said.

Lana uncrossed her arms. "Fine," she said. "*Once*. How are you going to get it, though? Kids our age aren't allowed to buy tickets."

"Don't worry, I have a plan for that," I said quickly, before they changed their minds. "And trust me, it won't be like your dad. This time, it's going to work."

Lana stared at me, hard. "Okay. And what if you do win? Will you quit Rock Reading?"

I took a step back. Somehow, I'd been so caught up dreaming about the money, I hadn't once stopped to wonder what I'd do afterward. Now that I did, I realized that of course we wouldn't *need* to keep Rock Reading. Obviously we'd stop, right? So why did the thought turn my insides to sludge?

I opened my mouth, then closed it again. Feather, stricken, filled the gap. "Of course you can't stop. This is your soul mission!"

Lana had gone very still.

I looked from her, over to our easel, and the poster promising to make wishes come true. And standing there, with the sun filtering through the treetops and a light, humid breeze blowing my frizz-curls, it hit me: Lana wanted to keep Rocking Reading with me.

Because she liked it.

And I did, too.

I *liked* being a Rock Reader.

I almost laughed out loud from the surprise of it. "I won't quit if you don't."

Lana's whole face broke into a smile, and Feather beamed up at me like I was her very own personal, short-tempered fairy godmother.

I grinned back at them. "I guess we've got work to do."

As if on cue, a couple of kids crossed into the park and headed our way.

The next few hours flew. Today, rather than zapping my energy, the Rock Readings seemed to feed it. Before I knew it, it was time for lunch. Lana handed out thermoses of icy lemonade, Feather grabbed almond-butter honey sandwiches out of her multicolored fabric hippie bag, and I explained my plan for how to get the lottery ticket.

When I finished, Lana shook her head. "You dragged our old babysitter into this? Is that even legal?"

"She's eighteen." I shrugged. "It's totally legal. I checked. All she has to do is give us the ticket as a 'gift,' then my mom can sign it and claim the money for us."

"And Adara agreed to this?"

"Well, I did have to promise her twenty percent of the winnings," I admitted. "But there will still be plenty left for us. Now, listen, promise you'll stay up to watch the results at eleven, since I can't." I paused. "Dang it, I can't even get texts. How will I know we won?"

"Oh, please," said Lana. "Can you imagine how excited my dad will be if we win? He'll drive me over in a second."

"Ooh, I want to come, too!" said Feather. "Liv will drive me for sure!"

I could practically feel cartoon stars in my eyes as I imagined all of us together, celebrating.

Feather clapped her hands together. "I can totally picture it. I'm starting to think you really can do this!"

Even Lana couldn't help but smile a teeny bit. I grabbed the cash box and pulled out a couple of twenties. "I'm supposed to go meet Adara now," I said. "And I want to get a bunch of candy and stuff, too, to celebrate."

Lana glanced at our line of customers. "I'll go. You stay here and do some more readings." Feather bounced out of her chair. "I'll go with. I can pull the wagon!"

Lana paused, raising an index finger. "We're getting one ticket. *One*. Then never again."

"Agreed," I said. After all, one was all I needed.

CHAPTER 35

My mood light as air, I got back to the Rock Readings. I finished two more fast and was about to motion my next customer over when I noticed the adorable little blond kid dragging his mother toward me through the grass.

"Joey!" I waved.

"No cuts!" shouted someone from the back of the line.

"I'm sorry," said Joey's mom, breathing a little hard as she approached the table. "This couldn't wait, apparently. He was insistent."

"Patience!" I shouted. Then I patted Joey's soft head. "Hey, little guy. I can't let you cut, but do you want to watch me do some Rock Readings?"

"No," he said, jutting out his lip and looking at the ground. "No wocks." Then he stuck a finger in his mouth and chewed it. "Deo no home."

"No, sweetie," said his mom, tucking a loose strand of hair behind her ear. "This isn't Geo's home."

"No!" he said, removing his finger and looking straight at me. "Deo no *doe* home."

"Sorry," she said again, looking embarrassed. "We really shouldn't be interrupting like this. Come on, sweetie, let's go wait in line."

But I was now intent on understanding what he meant. "No, it's okay . . . Joey, are you saying that you think I shouldn't go home?"

Joey nodded. "No doe home."

"Huh, weird," said his mom, looking at him thoughtfully. "Does that mean anything to you?"

I tore my eyes away from Joey's gooey little face. Why wouldn't he want me going home? Sure, I'd said Jade was evil. But she wasn't, like, *dangerous*, was she?

I must have sat there biting my lip too long, because Joey's mom went into worried-mom mode. "Sorry to pry, but is everything okay? Because if you're in any kind of danger, you need to talk to an adult, right away."

"Nah," I said, waving her off. "It's nothing like that. It's this aggravating girl staying with us. My mom's out of town and . . . it's a long story."

That only made Joey's mom even more worried. "I'd feel better if you talked to someone," she said. "Joey's rarely wrong. Is there someone you can talk to? Or somewhere else you could go until your mom gets back?"

I immediately thought of Liv's. My mom would never give me permission to sleep over there, not without meeting Liv first, and I couldn't ask anyway since I didn't have my phone. Not to mention Alan would be furious. On the other hand, how fun would that be? Maybe we could even talk Lana into staying, too. When the lottery results came in, we'd go absolutely nuts, probably jumping all over Liv's puffy couches and throwing popcorn in the air. Alan and my mom would definitely forgive me once they heard the news.

I squatted down to Joey's level. "Okay, buddy, you got it. I won't go home. I'll stay with my friend instead. You'd like her a lot. Her name is Feather!"

He beamed, looking as relieved as any two-year-old can. "Feather!"

"Well!" said his mom. "I'm glad to hear it. Honestly, I would have worried all night. Never a dull moment with this one!"

"He's some kid," I agreed. After waving goodbye, I turned back to my line of customers, but before I could call the next one over, I saw Lana and Feather coming toward me. What caught my attention was their expressions. They were straining as they dragged the loaded wagon over the bumpy grass, but this was more than just being red, panting, and sweaty from their midday walk. Something was wrong.

"You got the ticket, right?" I checked nervously.

"Yeah," panted Lana, pulling it out of her pocket and handing it to me. "Here, keep this safe. I took a picture, and so did Feather and Adara, so we all know the numbers and can watch the results. But, Geo, I checked my phone at the store, and you need to see this." Grimly, she wiped her forehead on her T-shirt, then held up her phone. The glare from the sun made it hard to see anything, but I could hear Jade's voice.

Feather was looking as annoyed as I'd ever seen her get. "She's accusing you of witchcraft again. Like that's even a bad thing."

"Well, she's accusing her of *dark* witchcraft," said Lana.

I rolled my eyes. "Who cares?" I gestured to our line. "She already tried that, but all it does is give us more business."

"But it's not just that." She held up her phone again. "Look. She's streaming live. Right now. *From your room.*"

"My WHAT?" I grabbed Lana's phone and sure enough, there was my dingy wall, yellowed lamp, and old brown carpet.

This was completely unacceptable. A total violation. I had to get her out of there. I tossed the phone back to Lana. "I've got to go."

"I'll come with," she said, always ready to be Sam to my Frodo.

"Me too!" said Feather, standing tall.

"No, you two stay here. I shouldn't be long. You can hand out the candy to keep everyone happy while I'm gone."

Lana wrinkled her forehead. "Are you sure?"

I should have paused then. I should have remembered Joey's warning, the warning he'd given me, like three seconds before. But my rage at Jade had blasted all the common sense out of me, so instead I said, "I'll be fine," and took off at full run.

"Put up a protection shield!" called Feather as I dashed out of the park.

A protection shield? I wasn't about to turn around and ask what the dunk *that* was.

Looking back, maybe I should have.

CHAPTER 36

Piece of free advice: If a psychic two-year-old begs you not to do something, don't do it. It's, like, horror movie 101, right alongside "don't split up," "don't open the door to the creepy basement," and "don't spend the night with five friends in the abandoned cabin in the woods next to the lake where that kid once drowned." Here's more free advice: Don't sprint under a midday sun during a summer heatwave unless you enjoy feeling like a dirty wet sponge having an asthma attack. By the time I'd reached my house and raced up three sweltering flights of stairs, I could feel the heat pulsing out of me with every heartbeat. I was panting so hard I could barely breathe and was, quite literally, dripping with sweat.

I burst into my room, knowing I looked completely unhinged. Jade was ready for me. She swiveled around with a gasp and a scream, all while holding her phone steady for a perfect shot. "It's the witch!"

"A+ for drama," I spat through my huffing. "Very good. We're all super impressed." Then I pointed back down the stairs. "Now GET OUT."

Jade smiled as she clicked off her phone. "I was only looking for evidence of devil worship. I felt it was my duty."

"How about you stealing my phone?" I seethed. "How many of your followers know about *your* dark side?" I was getting ready to unleash more of my fury on her when I was interrupted by Alan calling from below.

"Girls! That is enough! I want both of you in your own rooms. Now. And I want you to stay there."

Wait. Jade being sent to her room made perfect sense. But what did he mean by "both of you"?

"Alan, you can't possibly—"

"Yes, Geo, you too. You ran off this morning without telling me where you were going, knowing I couldn't reach you by phone."

"Yeah," I said, incensed. "Because she took it! And in case you didn't notice, she was just in here showing my bedroom to thousands of internet strangers. But by all means, sure, treat us like we're the same."

He shook his head at me. "This is not the Geo I know." Then he turned to Jade. "Come on. Give me your phone.

You're both grounded to your rooms for the rest of the day, no internet."

That was when my mind decided to replay Joey's warning. He'd been so worried. What if he was right? What if something bad was going to happen? "Alan, I—"

But he held up his hand again. "This is not up for discussion."

"But—"

"Look, I don't want to talk until we've all calmed down," he said. "Jade, come with me."

So much for my promise to Joey that I'd stay at Feather's. Jade shot me a smug smile as she headed out the door, and Joey's warning flared up again.

"Alan—" I tried one last time. He must have heard something in my voice, because he paused on the steps and glanced back, ready to listen.

But what could I say to him? That I needed to stay at Feather's because I'd been warned by a psychic two-year-old to stay away from my house? No way. "Just . . . something doesn't feel right. Please be careful, okay?" I finished lamely.

He gave me a quizzical look. "Of course. Don't worry. I've got this situation completely in hand."

CHAPTER 37

Alan, it turned out, did not have the situation in hand. He did not even have it in foot. But none of us knew that yet, so as he went down the stairs with Jade I tried to relax. After all, the ticket was bought, and that was the only thing that truly mattered. So, much as I wanted to torch Jade, I gave it a "cancel, clear, delete." She wasn't worth the waste of thought. Yes, it was infuriating to be grounded when I'd done nothing wrong, but it would be over soon. All I had to do was wait until eleven p.m. After that, my entire life was going to change, and every problem I had would be solved for good, Jade included.

I spent the time lounging on my bed, staring at the ceiling, lost in embarrassingly cheesy daydreams of being hoisted over the Jackson sisters' heads while they chanted about how amazing I am, and of Alan telling me I was right and sheepishly apologizing to me for not believing in the woo, and Lana telling me that I'm her hero as she and her dad moved into a brand-new, sparkling clean house.

With good old Fridgie keeping my room cool and my imagination playing movies in my head, time passed fast. At some point Alan knocked on my door with a couple slices of cheese pizza, a nice frosty Coke, and an apology. By that time I wasn't as angry anymore, and he seemed relieved that I wasn't in a fighting mood. So he went back downstairs and came back with another surprise: a plastic grocery bag bulging with Skittles, gummy worms, Twizzlers, and peanut butter cups. That was care of Lana and Feather, who had stopped by earlier to check in on me. He hadn't allowed them upstairs to say hi, but it was good of him to hand over the loot.

My belly full of cheese and sugar, I lay back down to wait out the last few hours. I hadn't even realized I'd fallen asleep until I lurched bolt upright in the dark.

I rubbed my eyes, disoriented. Something had woken me up, but what? That's when I heard it again. A faint creak that sent chills up my spine. Joey's warning sounded in my ears, making my heart thump. I wasn't in actual danger, was I? And what the heck time was it, anyway? Without my phone there was no way to tell. I knew it couldn't be past eleven yet; if it was, everyone would be here screaming and hollering.

I clicked on my nightstand lamp and checked that my door was still closed. It was, but somehow the dingy light made things feels even spookier than the dark. I was used to all the groans my old house made and I'd never felt scared in my room before. So why, when I heard yet another creak, did all my muscles tense?

For several minutes more all I heard was Fridgie, humming faithfully away. I was just beginning to relax, when I heard something else. Something worse. I looked toward the soft grinding noise and realized my doorknob was slowly turning.

I sat frozen as my door slowly opened, just a few inches, then stopped. In the crack, a hand appeared.

A hand with painted blue fingernails, holding a phone, which was pointed right at me.

Jade.

My fear vanished, replaced instantly with outrage. "What. The. JUNK." I flew out of bed and slammed my body against the door, hoping to catch her fingers and make her drop her phone. Instead, she snatched it back and snortled on the other side of the door with a note of triumph.

"You were going to record me *sleeping*?" I hissed.

"Oh, come on," she whispered. I could hear the eye roll in her voice. "Get a sense of humor. It was only a prank."

Gourd I hated her. "How do you even have your phone back? Where's Alan?"

"Oh, don't worry about Alan; he's snoring up a storm. I only came up because my fans demanded it."

I thunked my forehead against the door. No way was I going to give her the satisfaction of thinking I cared about her stupid followers.

"Yeah," she continued after I didn't reply. "They literally begged me to do it. They were sure you'd be doing something evil for the witching hour."

The witching hour? What the dunk was she talking about? Even though I knew she was 100 percent baiting me, I couldn't keep from asking. "The what?"

"The witching hour?" she repeated. "Three a.m.? They were sure we'd catch you mid-spell. Especially since it's also the Solstice."

I squeezed my eyes shut as if somehow that could stop the dread that was pooling in my stomach. Three a.m.? No. It couldn't be. Everyone would have been here by now. No way would they wait till tomorrow to tell me we'd won. They'd be over here making a huge scene.

I put my hands on the door. "Jade. What time is it?"

"I just told you, it's three a.m. If you don't believe me, why don't you check your phone?" I barely heard her cackle over the rushing sound filling my ears. "Oh! That's right. I forgot to tell you, I actually found it. Wait till you hear where! Seems you somehow dropped it . . ." She let out one last short, malicious bark of laughter. "In the toilet."

CHAPTER 38

I don't know how long I stood there with my hands against the door, but at some point I realized my entire body was shaking. I'd barely even registered what Jade had said at the end about my phone. My brain only had space for one, single, horrible, soul-sucking thought: There was no such thing as manifesting.

A Rock Reader, I thought with disgust as a giant rotting meatball of misery pushed itself up into my throat. How could I have been so dumb? How could I have fallen for all that feather-brained New Age woo-woo garbage?

I slowly slid to the floor. I wasn't magical at all. Alan had been right all along: Magic isn't real. What a fool I'd been, thinking I could control reality with a bunch of stupid rocks.

No, I was worse than a fool. I was a dried-up blood blister of a jerk. I was your grandmother's peeled off toe corn. No, I was your grandfather's stinking, infested carbuncle.

I was . . .

I was . . .

No.

WAIT.

I'd been duped. Not just by Feather and Liv, but by the whole friggin' universe. It had set me up with coincidence after coincidence, getting my hopes up, throwing so-called signs my way, turning my mind to mush. And I'd fallen for it, making a fool of myself in front of the whole world.

Just like that, all my shame and disappointment morphed into rage, a rage that punched through me like a fist. I felt it getting hotter and hotter, pressure building, until the urge to destroy something was almost too much to take.

I threw myself down on my bed and let the images flow. The very first one that came was Jade's face, hard as flint as she laughed and sneered at my failure. I flew at her in my mind, striking her over and over with my fists until, just like the rock, she began to throw off sparks. I watched as they showered out everywhere, falling to the ground like fiery rain.

But it wasn't enough. It wasn't nearly enough. Images of my house flashed in my head next. Horrible, ugly, falling-down house. I hated this stinking house. I despised it so much I wanted it to burn.

So that's what I did. I burned it. And this time I didn't cancel, clear, delete any of it. Why would I? It was all bunk! It was lies! I couldn't make things happen. If my mom got that job, we were moving, and there was nothing I could do about it. My visions were a big bunch of meaningless fantasies, and that's all.

It felt good to give in to my rage. I started in the laundry room, picturing my mom's so-called office with that falling-down card table she pretended was a desk. I imagined holding up a giant military-grade blowtorch and I hit that table with high-pressured jets of fire it until it smoked, warped, and melted. I watched with satisfaction as the computer slid off in a shower of sparks and exploded against the floor.

I did the kitchen next, blasting everything from the crusty old stovetop to the peeling linoleum floor and the walls the color of mold, until the only thing left to see was flame.

That felt even better. I went from the kitchen to the living room to the stairs, floating up like some kind of fire witch, with flames licking at my heels. I sent them to every room I passed, except my mom's. Finally, I reached my room. I saw good old Fridgie, and just like that, I was done.

When I opened my eyes, I was panting and shaking and covered in sweat, as if I'd woken up from a nightmare. I looked around my room, half expecting to see smoke, but all I saw was the real Fridgie, with his cool metallic sides and his low, steady hum.

I flopped back down, curled up in ball, and took a long, shuddering breath. No more fire, no more smoke, no more destruction. Just me and my faithful air conditioner, doing his best to cool me down.

Eventually I fell asleep again. And when I woke, my house was on fire.

CHAPTER 39

The screech of the smoke alarm blasted me awake. I bolted upright and immediately began to cough.

Smoke. Real smoke.

Panic pulsed through me. "Alan!" I screamed, running blindly to my bedroom door. "Fire!" When my hand touched the doorknob, I pulled it back with a gasp. I felt the surface of the door, and even the wood was hot. I tried to scream again, but fell into another fit of coughing instead.

My room was too dark to see, so I slid my hand along the wall for the light switch. Even the wall was hot. And the switch, when I found it, flicked up and down uselessly. Facts from boring fire-safety assemblies slotted into my brain. Facts like "an entire house can burn in less than twelve minutes," and "more people die from smoke inhalation than fire."

Behind the blare of the alarm, another sound got louder. Crackling.

I dropped to the floor, kept my head low, and scrambled to the window. By the time I got it open my entire body felt weak. I leaned out as far as I could, gasping for air. "Help!" I tried to scream, but my voice was a croak. I banged on the side of the house until my palms stung, trying to make as much noise as possible, but it was useless.

Dad, I thought desperately, pulling my T-shirt over my mouth, nose, and stinging eyes. *I need you. What should I do?*

Instantly, an image flashed by. White, long, and knotted... my fire ladder! Duh! My mom had stashed one in my closet when I moved into the attic and given me a whole lesson on how to use it.

After groping across the floor, and throwing shoes and rocks and heaps of clothes out of the bottom of my closet, there it was, covered in a layer of gritty dust. I yanked it out of its red canvas case, then crawled back, trying to remember what my mom had taught me.

My fingers found the two metal hooks, which latched easily to the sill. My relief when I dropped the rest out and watched it unfurl was short-lived. The moment I stuck my head out of the window I saw that it was far too short. Even if I climbed all the way to the bottom and dropped from there,

I'd be two stories high and could easily break something, or worse.

Then I remembered what my mom had said: This ladder wasn't meant for this window. It was supposed to lower me down to the roof of the porch. I turned. That was Fridgie's window.

Pulling that ladder back in took almost more energy than I had left. The smoke was now so thick it was like sticking my head in a pile of hot ash. Even belly crawling wasn't working anymore. When I got to Fridgie I pulled myself up and clung to his sides as a wave of dizziness and nausea almost knocked me right back down.

For the first time ever, Fridgie was warm to the touch. Somehow I managed to shove the window up as high as it would go, loosening his perch. Feeling like I was betraying a friend, I braced my hands and pushed.

He didn't budge.

Behind me, the crackling grew louder and a wave of heat passed over me. Somehow, I just knew, my door was about to explode.

"Dad!" I sobbed, collapsing against Fridgie. "Please! I don't want to die!"

Instantly, I felt two spots of gentle, cool pressure on my back, like two steady hands pressing into me, holding me up. I pushed again and this time the cool energy seemed to channel through my back, running all the way down to my arms, so that when I pushed again, Fridgie moved. And finally, after a long, awful groan, he dropped.

I didn't even hear him land. Instead, a roar of heat half pushed me out the window from behind, searing my back. Goodbye, bedroom door.

Smoke was everywhere now, pouring out the window all around me. Soot filled my eyes, blinding me as I tossed the end of the ladder out the window and fumbled the metal parts against the sill. The heat on my back forced me out farther and farther as I tried to make the hooks hold. I was so dizzy from coughing and my body felt so weak I didn't know how I'd be able hold on to the ladder, much less climb down.

"Dad!" I cried again, grabbing a side of rope in each hand and hoisting my legs over the sill.

I felt his hands on my back again, strong and firm, then heard him speak as clear as if I was listening to one of his videos. *Keep holding. One hand over the other. You can do this.* Blind and choking, I focused on nothing except his voice.

Slowly and methodically, we climbed down.

When I reached the end of the ladder. I held on to the bottom rung as hard as I could. I was dangling in midair, my useless eyes filling with tears as I kicked and stretched. I reached with my toes, trying to find solid ground, but all I felt beneath me was air and heat. If I let go, would I drop through a burning roof into an inferno?

A sob rose through my lungs and when I breathed in, all I got was more thick, black smoke. Sparkles of light filled my closed eyelids. "Dad!" I croaked, one last time. The sparkles condensed into a pinprick as the strength drained out of my hands.

I let go and the world went blank.

CHAPTER 40

I don't remember hitting the roof of the porch, or landing on my wrist. I don't remember the fire trucks coming or the paramedics strapping me into the ambulance. I definitely don't remember my house exploding as we drove away.

What I do remember, in a vague, fuzzy kind of way, is 1) throwing up a bunch of times into a blue plastic bin (ew), 2) having tubes stuck painfully up my nostrils and down my throat (ick), 3) having my wrist examined (ouch), and 4) having nurses cut off my clothes and scrub me all over with a rough cloth (embarrassing). I have other memories that feel more like dreams, of bright lights and various doctor-type people hovering over me and saying the kinds of things you usually only hear on medical dramas, things like "It's a miracle she made it out," and "This one's a fighter," and "You're going to be okay."

When I woke, my wrist hurt, my eyes ached, my lungs burned, and my throat felt like it'd been clawed by angry cats. And, I really, really, really wanted my mom.

I blinked tears away until my vision cleared. Three faces were peering down at me, lit from behind by fluorescent ceiling lights. None of them were my mom, but they were nearly the next best thing.

"I'm not dead, you know," I croaked, my voice sounding like it belonged to an eighty-year-old smoker.

Lana's entire face crumpled, big fat tears squeezing out through her shut eyes.

Feather, on the other hand, broke into a megawatt smile. "You're awake! Oh my god, it's a miracle you survived! A miracle!" She was talking a mile a minute, hardly stopping for breath. "They almost didn't find you—luckily they saw the rope ladder hanging down—I can't believe you climbed down that thing! You were totally knocked out and they almost didn't get you down in time and they were driving away when it exploded and you should see yourself, you look terrible!"

"Feather," said Liv, pulling her away. She tilted her head at Lana, who was sobbing into her hands.

"Oh no," said Feather. "Lana, I'm so sorry. I got overexcited. I didn't mean to—"

"Alan?" I croaked.

"Alan's okay," said Liv, as my eyes filled with tears of gratitude and relief. "They're treating him in another room, but he's going to be fine. Your mom is on her way right now, landing in a couple of hours. How about you? Do you need anything?"

I shook my head, then looked at Lana, who was crying like I was dead.

"Let's give these two a moment," Liv said to Feather.

Once we were alone, I attempted a grin. "I'm actually still alive over here, in case you didn't notice. You don't need to drip snot all over the place."

Lana sort of laugh-sobbed at that, grabbed about six tissues from the little tray next to my bed, and blew her nose into the giant wad. When she spoke, her voice was thick. "You almost died," she said. "Your house . . . it's like a horror movie, all jagged and charred. No one knew what happened to you, or where you were. I was so scared. I thought—"

She swallowed.

"You threw up, didn't you?" I said.

She smiled despite herself. "Right on your neighbor's mailbox."

"You should have barfed on Jade instead." She tried to laugh, but it turned into another round of sobs. As I watched her, horror dawned on me.

I could barely get the words out. "Lana, did I kill Jade?"

"What?" she asked, making a big wet honk on a fresh tissue. "No! She got out. She's fine. Why would you even ask that?"

I was glad to hear I hadn't mind-murdered Jade, but that didn't stop the ooze from creeping into my gut. "It was me, Lana. The fire was my fault."

Lana looked at me like maybe the smoke had given me brain damage. "It wasn't you. They're still looking into what caused it, but it started on the bottom floor."

"I manifested it, Lana. I pictured the entire thing, room by room."

Her eyes went wide.

"When we didn't win the lottery, I thought it meant I wasn't a manifester," I said feebly. "I was so mad I wanted to torch something, so I pictured the house burning. When I woke up, it was on fire."

"Whoa," she said. She twisted her braid for a few moments, frowning, then took a breath. "Okay, but you still can't take the blame. You were upstairs, and they said they think it started downstairs. You were asleep."

I shook my head, and when I tried to talk, a fresh fit of coughing got in the way. A nurse came through the door. "You need to rest those lungs, kiddo. Your friend can come back later."

I didn't want Lana to go, but I realized my head was pounding. "I'll come back as soon as I can," she whispered.

When she got to the door, she turned around. "It wasn't you."

I attempted a smile.

After she left, I fell into a miserable, nightmarish sleep. When I opened my eyes again, it wasn't Lana in the room with me. It was Liv.

CHAPTER 41

"Hey," I whispered hoarsely.

Liv sat next to me on the bed, her green eyes serious. "Are you well enough to talk?"

I nodded, but turned my head away. I knew exactly why she was there. "You're going to tell me it wasn't my fault. But it was."

She said nothing.

I turned my head back, needing to make her understand. "I manifested it, Liv. Every detail." I told her everything, then finished with, "I was so mad. I wanted to hurt someone, destroy something. I think something's wrong with me."

"Of course there's nothing wrong with you," she said gently. "We all feel that way sometimes. Everyone. It's part of being human."

"No, it's different for manifesters. The stuff I picture happens. Someone could have died last night."

She nodded, then pressed her lips together for a moment, thinking. When she spoke, she spoke carefully. "First of all, there's no way to know that you made that fire happen."

"But Liv," I said, frustrated. "It happened *exactly* like I pictured—"

She held up her hand. "Just because we believe in manifesting doesn't mean that coincidence doesn't happen. That's number one. Number two is that, from what Lana told me, you weren't believing in your powers last night. You weren't intending any harm. You were just letting off steam."

"Right. So, basically, it's not safe for me to get angry anymore."

"No," said Liv. "That's not it at all. Your anger is part of what makes you powerful. Your feelings, your passion, your conviction, your confidence; they're all part of it. Never push genuine feelings down. You just need to learn safe ways to express them, that's all. And that's not all you need to learn."

I sighed. "Like the fact that lotteries don't work."

"Hardly ever."

I huffed impatiently. "What the dunk, Liv. So I can manifest snakes and dead grandfathers and fires from hell, but not something useful like money? That makes no sense." If manifesting was a person, I'd punch it.

Liv held up her hands. "Again, I don't believe you had anything to do with that fire." She looked off into the distance for a moment, then continued, slowly. "Manifesting isn't storybook magic. You can't order it around, snap your fingers, and instantly get what you want. When you try to control real magic, that just pushes it away." She paused, checking to see that I was listening. "Personally, I think of it as a kind of living force. It likes to be respected, it needs to be free, and it loves to play. It chooses who to work through, and sometimes gives us what we envision, often in ways that delight and surprise us. Other times it gets stubborn and withholds, and who knows why."

I sat quietly, chewing on her words. When she put it that way, magic sounded a little bit like me.

"Take lessons with me," she said suddenly. "I'd love to teach you."

Tears welled up in my eyes as I realized how much I'd like that, and how much I had grown to like Liv herself. Then I remembered the problem. The big problem, the real problem, the problem that was 100 percent still there and hadn't been solved at all.

Suddenly, all the feelings of the last day caught up with me and spilled over and my face grimaced with the effort of stopping my tears. "I can't. We don't even have a house anymore. We're definitely moving now."

Liv stretched out her arms and I fell into them, not even trying to stop the tears anymore. I blubbered all over her shoulder as she hugged me tight. She smelled like lemonade and lavender.

When I was done, I pulled back and took some ragged breaths. "It's going to be okay," she said, unplastering one of my curls from my cheek. "We'll figure this out. I promise." I nodded, wiping my eyes on the sleeve of my hospital gown. "You know what I think might help for now?" she continued as she handed me a handful of tissues. "Ice cream."

I squeezed out a tiny smile. "I wouldn't say no to ice cream."

Roughly two seconds after she'd left the room, I heard footsteps pounding toward my room, in full sprint. Before I could even process what they meant, a streak of Mom shot into the room and into my arms.

CHAPTER 42

I was hit at full mom speed, but gently. "My scorched little Rat Tail," she wailed, cupping my face in her hands. Then she smoothed my hair back, kissed my forehead about a thousand times, and inspected me all over. "You look like something a chimney coughed up. And your wrist! Are you hurting? Are you okay? Oh thank god, thank god, thank god." She clutched at me like I might disappear, rocking me back and forth. It made me feel like I was a baby again, which was exactly what I needed. Curling into her chest, I let her squeeze me until my hug tank was full.

"Tell me everything," she said as she pet my hair. So I did, just like I'd told Liv, except this time I included the part about the hands on my back. "It was Dad," I said, needing her to believe. "I know it was. I heard him. He was there."

"I believe you," she said, hugging me all over again. But when we pulled away, her face had fallen. "Geo, I'm so sorry I left you." She dropped her head into her hands. "Oh, god. I'm so sorry."

"Mom," I said, shaking her shoulder. "Stop it. This wasn't your fault." I choked as a fresh wave of sobs rose up. "It was me, Mom. I burned our house. Dad's house."

She shook her head. "No, Geo, it wasn't. The investigator called, and she said the cause was old wiring. The fire started on its own in the laundry room."

"But you don't understand," I said. "It was me. I pictured it—"

She put her hands on my face and looked in my eyes. "Did you hold a match? Did you at any point use an actual blowtorch?"

"No, but . . ."

"You didn't do anything whatsoever to start that fire, except imagine it. You pictured it in your mind, and that's it. Correct?"

"Yes, but I'm a manifester and—"

"Doesn't count. I'm sorry, but even if you're the most powerful manifester on earth, I'm not letting you own this. I don't care if you read a step-by-step manual titled *How to Burn Your House Down with Your Mind*, I'm still saying it's not your fault."

"Are you saying you don't believe in manifesting?"

"That's not what I said." She took a breath. "Okay, so it seems to me like this manifesting doesn't always work, right? No matter how good you are, it's never going to be a hundred percent. Not even you. So if the things you picture sometimes come true and sometimes don't, then clearly there's more to it. Something more than just your intention."

"Liv thinks magic is like a living thing," I said. "That it chooses."

She shrugged. "Magic, god, angels, fate, the universe. Who knows? 'There are more things in heaven and earth, Horatio, than are dreamt of in your philosophy.'"

Before I could ask her what the heck a Horatio is, Liv poked her head around the door. "Did I just hear Shakespeare?"

My mom laughed as Liv emerged into the room holding two plastic bowls. "I hope I'm not intruding? I come bearing ice cream."

"No," said my mom, standing up. "Please, come in. I'm Rae. You must be Liv? I believe I owe you a thank-you. A huge one." She wiped away a fresh tear. "Thank you for being here."

Liv's smile went so megawatt that her freckles almost seemed to glow. "My pleasure. You've got a wonderful kid." She handed me a chocolate vanilla twist, complete with a little wooden spoon and a cherry on top. "Feather's bringing some of her clothes for you to wear. You two are about the same size, I think?"

I had been about to take a giant bite of the ice cream, but stopped with the spoon halfway to my mouth. "Uh, thank you, but . . ." I trailed off, sending my mom a *help!* look. Hippie skirts and fitted tank tops? Not me, not ever.

And maybe telepathy is another woo-woo thing that's real, because my mom grinned like she somehow knew exactly what I was thinking. "No need for that," she said. "There's a store two blocks down with plenty of grubby shorts and oversized T-shirts. I can be there and back in a jiff."

"Thanks, Mom. After that, are we allowed to go—"

I stopped short. I had been about to say "go home." But we no longer had a home. Where exactly were we supposed to go? We couldn't afford a hotel, and aside from Alan, my mom didn't have any close friends. It was hardly as if we could stay at Lana's house. "Where will we go?" I croaked.

"You're coming to my house, of course," said Liv definitively.

"Oh no," said my mom, holding up her hands. "We couldn't—"

"It's not up for discussion," said Liv. "We have plenty of space and we'd love the company. I insist."

"So do we!" shouted Feather, bursting through the door mid-clap, with Lana on her heels. "Please?! You *have* to come. Lana's staying, too. It'll be like an endless sleepover party! It'll be so fun!" She was jumping up and down so hard her long skirt was billowing beneath her. "Please please please! For real if you say no, you will *kill* me!"

"You must be Feather," said my mom, laughing despite herself. "And if it means that much to you, then I suppose we can't refuse."

"Thank you!" squealed Feather. Behind her, Lana beamed.

I looked from Feather to Lana to Liv to my mom, and sighed a big, happy sigh. Then, before I took a bite, I made sure to ask my mom if we could see Alan before we left.

"Of course," she said. "He's going to want to see you, too."

That settled, I closed my eyes, took a giant spoonful of ice cream, and savored the cool, creamy sweetness as it slid down my throat.

CHAPTER 43

After a few more tests and a dinner of applesauce, Jell-O, and gloppy meat substance, I was officially released from the hospital. But before we left for Liv's, my mom and I had to see Alan. I went in first.

I stepped into his room slowly, peeking around the curtain in case he was asleep. But he was just lying on the hospital bed with his hands at his sides, blinking at the ceiling. He looked pale, paler even than usual, and strangely small. Worst of all was the tube in his nostrils, connecting his lungs to a large tank by his bedside.

He saw me and turned his head, opening his mouth to talk, but immediately curled up in a horrible, long cough, worse than any of mine.

Tears came to my eyes. It was horrible, absolutely horrible, seeing him like that. "I should let you rest," I said quickly. But he shook his head so hard it made him cough even worse, so I waited. Tears were streaming from his eyes and I wasn't sure if it was from coughing or crying or both.

"I'm so sorry," he croaked out once he could. His voice sounded way worse than mine.

"Don't say that! It's not your fault."

His throat moved up and down like he'd swallowed a golf ball. "You could have died," he said. His tears came harder, and this time I knew it was not just from the coughing.

I gave his hand a squeeze. "But I didn't." I thought about telling him about my dad, how he saved me, and all the rest, but decided he didn't need to hear about any of that, at least not right now. "Look," I said instead. "I'm doing way better than you." I held up the arm with the cast on it. "They're letting me go, and I get to take this cool cast with me."

He tried to smile, but it was painful to see. Poor Alan. He was never going to babysit teenagers again.

"I know what you need," I said. I got up, left the room, and brought back my mom. I closed the door softly behind me while they hugged and hugged. When they called me back in, he seemed a little more cheerful, but only by a fraction. "He blames himself." My mom sighed as we headed back down to the hospital lobby. "Just like you blame yourself and I blame myself. I think humans do that because it makes us feel in control."

I chewed on that for a bit, then understood exactly what she meant. "Because we'd rather feel guilty than powerless."

She looked at me with pride. "You're a smart kid, you know that?" I smiled, but made a mental note to do a lot more thinking later. The fire had made me believe in manifesting again, but it was going to take a lot of time to sort out where the line was between what I could control and what I couldn't.

Walking out of the hospital felt like stepping into a whole different season. The hot weather had finally broken and with the sun getting low I could almost smell Fall in the air. Once we got to Liv's, she and Feather gave me, my mom, and Lana the official grand tour. I'd seen the first two floors before, of course, but not the rest. My mom gushed the whole way through, just like I knew she would. "It's like *Architectural Digest* in here!"

"And so clean," sighed Lana as we headed upstairs. I gave her arm a secret squeeze.

Feather's room was exactly what you'd guess: an explosion of beads, crystals, tie-dye scarves, lava lamps, and fairy figurines against a backdrop of lilac walls. Liv's room was about a thousand times more chill, an oasis of muted desert colors and as neat and organized as my mom's wildest dreams. "Gorgeous," said my mom, staring from the polished wood floors to the Buddha statue in the corner.

Liv just smiled, then led us to the top floor, which had not one guest bedroom, but three, each with a ginormous bed and more pillows than any human would ever need in a lifetime.

The sun was setting through the windows, casting a soft glow on every surface.

"You realize the danger you're in, here?" asked my mom, gazing at a vase of fresh sunflowers. "We may never leave."

Liv laughed. "This whole floor is yours for as long as you need it, and I mean that. Feather, come help me with the bags. Geo, are you hungry or would you rather rest?"

I could've eaten more after the hospital "dinner," but suddenly I was so exhausted I could barely stand. "I could use some sleep," I admitted. "But I do have one request."

"Name it," said Liv.

"Oreo pancakes in the morning?"

My mom raised an eyebrow.

"Dessert for breakfast," explained Liv. "Specialty of the house. And yes, you can count on it."

Everyone clattered down the polished wood steps except me and my mom. She shooed me into the sunflower bedroom, pulled down the coverlet, then patted the cool, crisp sheets. Even they were pretty, a bright yellow to match the rest of the room. I crawled in and sunk my head deep in the fluffed pillow. "I never asked about your interview."

"Tomorrow," she said, kissing my forehead.

"Please don't make us move from here," I said, blinking tears.

"I don't want to go either, Fart Face," she said sadly.

"Good. Then let's don't."

Her sigh was something I felt more than I heard. "Let's see if they give me the job first. No sense worrying about it till then."

I was too tired to argue, too tired to think, even too tired to feel. "Maybe you won't get the job. Maybe they hated you," I mumbled, feeling like I was sinking all the way through the mattress and into the earth.

She gave a tiny laugh. "We'll know soon enough."

My eyelids made a decision to close, and I didn't try stop them. I didn't have enough energy left to do anything except be. And in that moment, with my mom beside me and Liv's soft bed under me, just existing was enough.

CHAPTER 44

The next morning, I woke to whispers.

"Do you think she's awake?"

"It doesn't seem like it."

"But her eyelids moved."

"That's called REM. We should let her sleep."

"She wouldn't want to miss breakfast."

"She's got plenty of time. Liv and Rae aren't even back from the store yet."

I cleared my scratchy throat. "If you're going to argue about whether to wake someone up, you probably shouldn't do it six inches from their face. And stop looking at my eyelids, please."

"Oops," whispered Feather. "Sorry."

"I told you we should let her sleep," said Lana.

"She slept thirteen hours! I would think that's enough."

Thirteen hours? I opened my eyes and stretched. Feather was right, it was enough. Aside from my throat and my aching wrist, I felt about a thousand times better than I had in the hospital. I scooched up to the top of the bed, smiled to show I'd been kidding, then flopped back against one of Liv's ten thousand pillows and sighed. "I want to stay here forever."

"Tell me about it," said Lana, sitting by my feet.

"Then do!" gushed Feather, bouncing next to me, her hair escaping in little wisps from beneath a pink and purple tie-dye bandana. "You're only, like, the number one most talented manifester on the entire planet. So manifest it!"

"It's not like I didn't already try," I said, flushing with frustration. "That's why I bought that stupid lottery ticket, remember?" I looked guiltily at Lana. "Which was a huge fail, obviously. You were completely right, and I promise to never do it again as long as I live."

Lana crossed her arms and tried to hide her smile. "You'd better not."

"I warned you lotteries don't work," Feather said. "You were focusing on the how, not the what. Money is the how. You have to focus on what you *truly* want."

"But what if I truly want money?" I asked stubbornly.

"Nobody just wants money," she said, just as stubbornly. "It's what money *gets* you that matters. So forget about the money. Just think about what you'd do with it, and go straight to that."

I was starting to understand, even if I hated to admit it. "Fine. I'd stay in this town, in a house exactly like this, with you guys. And no stupid Jade living anywhere nearby," I added after a pause.

"That's exactly what I want, too," said Lana.

"Exactly, except cancel, clear, delete the part about Jade," said Feather. "You have to focus on what you want, not on what you don't want. Besides, you already got her out of your life. You manifested it, remember? I can't believe we nearly forgot to tell you. It turns out she really is going to California."

"Whoa." I patted myself on my back with my good hand. "Good job, me." It was never going to get old, finding out when my visions came true. "Okay, so let's just say I want to live in a house exactly like this one, one that my mom loves. And I also want my mom to have a job that she loves. And I want Alan to be happy again, too. But most of all I want to *stay*. Here, in this town, with you. *Both* of you," I added, surprised to realize how much I meant it.

"None of that actually has anything to do with money," said Lana thoughtfully.

"Exactly," said Feather, pink with happiness.

A last tiny gasp of protest came from what was left of my rational side. "But we *do* need money. That's the whole reason we're . . ."

"Stop!" Feather commanded. "Every time you focus on money, you block the magic. Just imagine the life you want and let the magic give it to you in its own fun way."

I blinked at her several times. What she was saying would make no sense at all to an Alan-type person. An Alan-type person would roll his eyes and think your brains had turned to mush.

But if you are the kind of person who believes magic is real, and that we can make things happen with our thoughts and beliefs... If you are, in other words, a thoroughly, deeply, completely woo sort of person, then it makes all the sense in the world.

"Lana," I said. "We're going to need some rocks."

CHAPTER 45

Maybe that zircon I'd used to talk to my dad a thousand years ago was still working its magic, because my idea was brilliant. I 100 percent knew it was going to work. I could already feel the chills forming.

"This Rock Reading is for us, Lana. Both of us. We'll do it together."

Lana's dark eyes took on light. "You choose the rocks," I continued. "I'll have the vision."

Feather squealed. "A Rock Reading for the Rock Readers! This is so going to work."

Lana grabbed her backpack and pulled out rock after rock, forming them into a grid on Feather's floor. "This feels so weird, choosing myself," she said, once she was done. "I love all my rocks. How do I pick?" She stared at the grid, thinking. Finally, she looked up. "Can I pick three?"

"Of course," I said. We'd only ever done two rocks before, but did it really matter? If Lana wanted three rocks, she'd get three rocks.

"Good," she said. "Because I'm choosing one for each of us."

I'm pretty sure Feather emitted actual sunbeams, hearing that. "Ooh! You're picking one for me, too?"

"You're part of this," Lana said. "We both want Geo to stay, and Geo and I both want you to stay, too."

Feather was practically levitating with delight. "That's what I want, too! To stay here with you both, and Liv, and never go back to California again. And I know my mom will let me, if I ask." She turned to me and continued in a rush. "So what are you going to pick? Something shiny, right? Or aquamarine? I'm Pisces, of course, so that would make sense. Or, no, maybe something colorful, or one that glows in the dark?"

Lana smiled, then picked up a plain, rough, circular sandy-brown lump. "You're pumice."

Feather blinked.

I didn't even try to hide my laugh. "Like what old people rub on their feet to get their corns off?"

Feather crossed her arms. "Very funny, Geo." She turned to Lana. "And why am I a foot scrubber, exactly?"

"Pumice is awesome," said Lana, looking offended on behalf of the little brown rock. "It's lava that gets shot out of a volcano, super high into the atmosphere. See all these little holes? Those are air bubbles. It's the lightest rock on the planet. Look." She got up and dropped it into the water glass on my bedside table. "It's the only rock that floats!"

Feather eyed it. "A rock that floats? I guess that's sort of cool?"

"Sometimes tiny little sea creatures use it as a life raft," said Lana.

Feather's smile returned. She plucked the pumice out of the water and dried it on her patchwork skirt. "A floating life raft, that sounds better. But you're sure I'm not, like, a sapphire or something?" The hopeful look on her face didn't last long.

"Definitely not," said Lana. "Those are hard and tough, and much too orderly. Pumice has no structure to it at all."

Feather grinned. "I like that. Pumice it is."

"You next," said Lana, considering me thoughtfully. She stared at the grid awhile, frowning. Then she reached out and grabbed her backpack. "I know exactly the right one . . . I think I . . . yes! Here it is." She held up a dull, round lump that was a little like Feather's pumice, minus the frothy bubbles.

"Ha!" said Feather. "You're as ugly as me."

"Not ugly at all," said Lana. "Outside, you're rough and hard and scratchy. But inside . . ."

"Ooooooh!" said Feather as Lana put one hand on either side and pulled, gently. It came apart into halves, each half filled with sparkling crystals. "A geode!"

Lana nodded, then put the rock back together and handed it to me. "It's celestine. Celestine is the major ore of strontium, used to make fireworks."

I half grinned, half grimaced. A geode with the potential to explode and cause fire? That was my rock all right.

"I'm a little jealous," said Feather, shaking hers near her ear. "I don't suppose there are secret crystal fireworks hidden inside of mine?"

"Nope. Just more air bubbles." Lana laughed.

Feather crossed her arms. "Hmph."

I stifled my own laugh, then turned to Lana. "What's yours going to be?"

She chose quickly, picking up a small, rusty lump with sides like a multisided die. "Garnet," she said, holding it out for us to see. "When I was little my dad took me panning at this mining place, and I got a big garnet. The guy in the shop said they're usually found in big hunks of messy rock, but the gem itself is perfectly ordered and structured. It's also extremely resistant. Once it's formed, it always stays the same. I've thought of it as my rock ever since."

"Stubborn, ordered, beautiful, and found in a big mess? Yup, it's you all right," I said, impressed. "Okay, we have our rocks. Now it's my turn."

I held all three rocks together in my hand, closed my eyes, and pressed them against my heart. The room was still bright, fresh, and filled with sunshine and flowers, but Lana and Feather had gone quiet and serious, giving it almost the feeling of a church.

A familiar shiver of energy ran through me as my vision formed. I saw me, Feather, and Lana exactly as we were now, sitting in a circle on the wood floor of Liv's guest bedroom. But in my vision, my mom, Liv, and Alan were there, too, hovering behind us like guardian angels. Colorful, dancing ribbons of light began to wind around us, growing brighter and longer until they weaved a shining dome around us.

"Together forever," I said inwardly, repeating it like a chant. I kept going, holding the vision sharp and clear, until I knew 100 percent without one whiff of doubt that it was going to happen. Or, no, not that it was *going* to happen; it *already had* happened.

At that moment of knowing, all the bubbles of happiness that had been filling my insides shot up and overflowed out the top of my head like carbonated soda. My eyes popped open and I was half surprised when the whole room wasn't filled with all the light I'd seen.

"Whoa," Lana gasped. "I actually felt that."

"That made my toes tingle." Feather sighed, her face shining. "How do you *do* that?"

"Don't ask me." I grinned, feeling lighter than the pumice stone. "I just make this stuff up."

That, for some reason, sent us sprawling on the floor in a fit of helpless giggles. "I don't get it," gasped Lana. "What's so funny?"

"I don't think we're laughing because it was funny," said Feather, wiping her eyes. "We're laughing because we're happy. Because we know it worked."

I rolled onto my back and let out a long, satisfied sigh. She might still be Feather-brained, but sometimes that girl was right.

CHAPTER 46

An hour later my belly was as warm and happy as the rest of me as we all sat around the table like a bunch of fat, satisfied cats.

"I wouldn't have thought to pair chocolate cookies and frosting with butter and maple syrup, but dang, it works," said my mom, sitting back in her chair with a moan.

"It almost makes you want to stay forever, doesn't it?" said Liv. And was it my imagination, or did she wink at my mom?

I sat up a little straighter and watched as my mom hid a smile. She noticed me staring, and sighed. "All right, Slug Breath, you're going to figure it out anyway. Liv offered me a job last night. She invited us to live here, *just* while I create a new website for Incense and Sensibility."

Next to me, Lana caught her breath. Feather let out one of her patented Feather squeals. "You make websites? We did it! You can stay! I knew it would work!"

"Hold on, now," said my mom, holding up her hand. "I haven't said yes."

Feather didn't stop squealing. "Oh you are *so* going to stay. It's for sure! Geo manifested it."

Liv cut in gently. "Feather, Lana, come downstairs. I need some help in the shop."

Lana, her face a mix of hope and worry, stood up to go. Feather, on the other hand, didn't even stop for a breath. "You *must* say yes. Aunt Liv's been needing a better website for ages, and she'll pay you whatever you want. *Anything*. No kidding, she's loaded!"

"Feather!" snapped Liv.

But Feather kept talking. "It's true! Our whole family is. My grandfather? He trademarked the smiley face, back in 1971. See? This is an original, all the way from France." She pointed to the wall, where a yellow smiley face HAVE A NICE DAY button was framed. "It makes *tons* of money, honest!"

Liv grabbed Feather in a pretend choke hold and dragged her toward the steps. I just stared, my mouth hanging open.

"This is *so* going to happen!" called Feather as she thumped down the steps.

"For the last time, hush!" I heard Liv hiss as they opened the door to the shop.

My mom and I sat alone in the kitchen, blinking at each other.

"That was . . ." she started. Then she shook her head to clear it and ran her fingers through her hair. "Okay, look, Goober Face. Liv is incredibly kind and generous—"

"And apparently insanely rich," I said, still trying to digest that fact.

"—and creating her website would be fun," she continued, ignoring me. "But it's a side gig at best. It's not a real job, with benefits and all the rest. I like Liv a lot, but I barely know her, and I will not take her charity. As soon as that website is done, we'd be back in the same boat as before."

"Not the same boat," I pointed out. "We'll be living here."

She glanced around and held up her hands. "I get it. This is the house of our dreams, and Liv has made us feel very welcome. But I can't live off someone else, no matter how nice or rich they are. If I accepted Liv's offer . . . it would diminish me."

As I listened to my mom, I noticed something strange. Instead of feeling upset or panicked, like I had to argue or convince her to stay, I felt curiously, deeply unworried.

"I'm sorry. I just can't do it," she finished. "I refuse to be dependent again."

I nodded. "I get that. It's okay. I would feel the same way."

My mom looked at me like I'd grown a third head. "You're not going to fight me on this? Aren't you mad?"

"No, I'm feeling pretty good, actually."

She squinted at me hard. "Are you saying you're okay with us moving?"

"Nope. It's just that I know we're not going to." It was the truth. Maybe I didn't know how it would happen or when it would happen, but I trusted my magic completely. We were going to stay here with Liv, Lana and I were going to keep Rock Reading at least for the rest of the summer, and I'd keep up the manifesting magic for the rest of my entire life. We were going to live the lives of our dreams, all of us. I was certain of it.

At that moment, my mom's phone rang. "It's the job," she said, looking back at me like I was pulling a prank. She pressed Talk and walked quickly to the far corner of Liv's sunroom. "I'm sorry, could you repeat that?" I heard her say. She glanced at me, her face puzzled, then turned the corner so I couldn't hear anymore.

I sprinted down the steps and motioned Liv, Feather, and Lana to come back upstairs. By the time we had piled back into the kitchen, my mom was standing there blinking and shaking her head. "I don't understand. You couldn't possibly have known. No one could have known."

My heart skipped a beat. "We're staying." It wasn't a question.

"They offered me the job . . ." she said, halfway in a daze. "Remotely. After they specifically said they wouldn't. They changed their minds, just like that, for no reason at all. I didn't even have to ask."

"Like, wait, so you can work from here?" Feather asked, clearly getting ready to squeal.

"Assuming you still want temporary roommates?" asked my mom, turning to Liv. "We'll pay full rent, obviously."

Liv's green eyes shined so bright her entire face seemed to glow. "The roommate offer is definitely still open."

Feather let loose her squeal and flung her arms around me. "We're going to be like *sisters*!"

Her hair wisped all over me, tickling my face and smelling like tangerines.

"Sisters?" I choked out. I sent Lana a joking *help!* look, but she just opened her arms wide and added herself to our hug. I realized she was shaking, and that's when it hit me for real. "We're staying. We did it."

Feather called to Liv and my mom, "Come on, you two, get in here. Group hug!" For the next minute or so I could hardly breathe for the weight of arms squeezing all around me. When we finally pulled apart, my mom was breathless. "This calls for a celebration. How about a Grrrls Date tonight?"

"New and improved Grrrls Date," I said, impersonating a commercial announcer. "Now with more girls."

As everyone bustled downstairs, I held back for a moment to take a closer look at the smiley face hanging on the wall. Who would've guessed a little thing like that could create such massive wealth? One week ago I would've plucked out my own toenails for that kind of fortune. But things had changed. I had changed. I used to believe that money was the answer to everything. Now I knew money wasn't the answer at all. The real answer was magic.

And I had plenty of that.

ACKNOWLEDGMENTS

Is it normal for first-time authors to get embarrassingly enthusiastic in their acknowledgments? I hope so, because that's what's about to happen here. To be fair, before becoming an author I had no idea how many people's work, creativity, expertise, and effort goes into the shaping of a single published book. Frankly, it's unfair that my name alone graces the cover.

The person who most deserves their name alongside mine is my amazing editor, Catherine Frank. New writers often mistakenly assume that editing is about surface polishing, things like refining sentences, perfecting punctuation, and other detail tweaking. True professional editing is a different beast altogether. It reaches its claws deep into the meat and marrow of a story, reworking characters, plot, structure, theme. . . . After a bout with a genuine editor, your story may be changed all the way down to its essence. Some of

Catherine's rewriting requests were so bold I'm surprised my eyebrows are still attached to my forehead. But thank goodness I trusted her, because somehow, mysteriously, instead of changing this book into something else, she made it into something more itself. From me and Geo both: Thank you.

None of this would have been possible in the first place were it not for my fabulous agent, Ginger Knowlton of Curtis Brown Ltd. She was my dream agent long before she was my actual agent, and is everything I could've wished for. The fact that she represents me now is enough all on its own to make me believe in the magic of manifesting. The unexpected frosting on the Ginger cake was her talented and insightful editorial assistant, James Farrell, who was himself responsible for early rounds of astute and incisive editing. Thank you both, so much!

To Susie Wilde: There's a reason this book is dedicated to you. The fact that multiple writers in your group have since been published is all anyone needs to know about your talents as a writing teacher. What's astonishing is that you're an even better friend. What a difference you've made to me, to all of us! And how lucky we all are to have you in our lives.

To all the Wilde writers who've been my critique partners through the years: Thank you, thank you, thank you! First and foremost, my "Tuesday" writing group: Samantha Corte, Charlotte Hord Smith, and Maripat Metcalf. You lot are there for me not just on Tuesdays, but every single day, as fellow creators and first-rate friends. You've read this manuscript so many times I've lost count. Even better, you've been there to crack me up and back me up, time and time again. There's not enough chocolate in the world to express how much I appreciate you.

To all my other Wilde friends: To Adrea Theodore, who's walked the publishing path alongside me, I'm so grateful for your encouragement, support, and commiseration. To Jeanne Stadel, Lynden Harris, Nancy Phifer, Olivia "Liv" Florence Davis (if the name sounds familiar, there's a reason), Julie Fortenberry, Diane Judge, Amanda Lee Scherle, Annie Runyon, Jen Kelley, Kamie Edwards, Lucy Rozier, Gwinn Ward, and many, many more: I cannot think of a single critique session where I didn't come away with either my manuscript greatly improved, or, quite often, myself.

To Ellen Manning, teacher extraordinaire! You were that person in my life, that wondrous person every writer can point to, who first made me believe that my dreams might actually be possible. You didn't only instigate my journey as a writer, but *Geo's Fortune* was quite literally born in your classroom. How can I possibly thank you and your class full of Meerkats enough for that?

To Carl Quesnel of the Boston Mineral Club: Thank you so much for your rock and mineral expertise, for all the work you're putting into the Rock Readers website, and for being one of my oldest friends to boot. Your knowledge, skill, and general all-around good-naturedness has been, and will always be, invaluable.

Finally, to my family: Mom and Dad, thank you for a lifetime of unwavering love and support. My mom, it should be noted, bears no resemblance of any kind to Geo's mom, but is just as fierce in her own inestimable way. Last but not least, my husband, Peter, and my kids, Ben and Charlotte: There's no possible adequate way to thank you, so I'm not going to try. It's enough that you know that I know that you've made me the luckiest person in the world.

Thank you!

About the Author

AMY B. MUCHA spent her childhood gobbling up books, dreaming up stories, and wandering the woods in search of magic. She feels wildly lucky to have settled in Hanover, New Hampshire, with her husband and a houseful of pets. Amy still spends her time gobbling up books, dreaming up stories, and wandering the woods, only now she knows there's magic in the world for sure. She invites you to visit her at *AmyBMucha.com* and to find some luck and magic of your own at *RockReaders.com*.